November 2001

Dr. Swarthmore

Pam —

I'm not sure at this point what it means, if anything, but here it is.

Best,

Julian

Erratum

Insert the following words before "justified" in the first line of page 58:

"phonographs and sewing machines, whose cost could be"

Dr. Swarthmore

Alexander Scala

The Porcupine's Quill

NATIONAL LIBRARY OF CANADA CATALOGUING IN PUBLICATION DATA

Scala, Alexander, 1944–
Dr. Swarthmore

ISBN 0-88984-228-0

I. Title.

PS8587.C34.D62 2001   C813'.54   C2001-901618-2
PR9199.3.S2545D62 2001

Published by The Porcupine's Quill
68 Main Street, Erin, Ontario NOB 1T0
www.sentex.net/~pql

Readied for press by John Metcalf; copy-edited by Doris Cowan.
Typeset in Bauer Bodoni, printed on Zephyr Antique laid,
and bound at The Porcupine's Quill Inc.

Represented in Canada by the Literary Press Group.
Trade orders are available from General Distribution Services.

We acknowledge the support of the Ontario Arts Council,
and the Canada Council for the Arts for our publishing program.
The financial support of the Government of Canada
through the Book Publishing Industry Development Program
is also gratefully acknowledged.

1 2 3 4 • 03 02 01

Canada

For Justine and Clelia

Table of Contents

What vulgar criticism would call grossly material success really involves a feat of creative imagination in certain respects more wonderful than any other known to human experience; for while the creative artist is bound only to imitate the divine imagination which controls the universe, the man who achieves practical success is bound so to share that divine imagination as for a while even to share, too, the prophetic foresight of divinity.

Barrett Wendell, *William Shakespere* (1895)

The Pamphlet

Dr. Swarthmore presided over a sectarian college in rural Indiana. He had, as well, the charge of a small church in the adjacent village – though the church was not so small (and this was his favourite joke) that his congregation ever filled it. He had been briefly married, long a widower. In the last autumn of the nineteenth century, he published a visionary pamphlet. Its title page was laid out as follows:

THE PLAN OF GOD
As Revealed to His Servant, George Kennicott Swarthmore, D.D.
BEING
an account of the manifestation to Dr. Swarthmore
of a *Celestial Herald*
bearing to mankind Good News of the imminence of

JESUS CHRIST

and

a full, faithful and accurate transcription of the speech
that passed between the *Herald of God* and *Dr. Swarthmore*
(as sworn and attested to by NINE WITNESSES
of proven character and probity)
on the twenty-first day of September in the year
NINETEEN HUNDRED

WITH some particulars of Dr. Swarthmore's VISION
of
A TRANSFIGURED WORLD
of peace, order and justice

ten cents

Opposite the title page stood a half-tone portrait of Dr. Swarthmore himself, a stout, elderly man with a dense beard and large teeth. The teeth were visible because Dr. Swarthmore's mouth was slightly ajar and his rubbery underlip was turned down, an arrangement that caused him to look astonished or, at least, gravely perplexed. The appearance of astonishment, with its implication of vulnerability or credulity, was contradicted by the bony prominence of the Doctor's brows, which were configured in a scowl. The brows conveyed truculence and pride of intellect. The eyes, however, did not verify the report given by the brows. The eyes were mild. They were very pale, with irises that were scarcely distinct from the whites.

A second half-tone, midway through the pamphlet, showed the Nine Witnesses mentioned on the title page. The Witnesses stood close together against an empty background – so close together that they appeared to be holding each other up. All nine wore beards and overalls, and all of their eighteen eyes were glassy and opaque. The Witnesses looked like taxidermy. The facing page offered a facsimile of the document that embodied their common testimony. Below the text stood their signatures, written in a variety of unpractised hands. All of the signatures, like the testimony itself, were completely illegible.

This is what the pamphlet had to say:

On the evening of the twentieth of September, a little after dark, Dr. Swarthmore was called to the bedside of one of the elders of his church. The Doctor received this summons (the pamphlet did not say by what agency he received it) as he was eating a solitary supper in the kitchen of his parsonage. He took up a few more peas on the blade of his knife, then pushed himself away from the table. He rolled down his shirtsleeves and put on his coat of well-brushed black broadcloth. He took a cigar from the inside pocket of the coat and lit it. When he stepped out of the house he noted the mildness of the evening air, the roundness of the catalpa tree in the yard. He stepped out amid the hosannas of the katydids.

Dr. Swarthmore drove his trap through the village, escaped its circumscription of trees and entered the level and nearly featureless countryside – the profound Indianian flatness and openness, which always presents to the mind's eye some bump or tilt or dimple that isn't there, because the mind rejects that absolute flatness, can't or won't sustain it. Neither the Doctor nor his horse was in a hurry. They sniffed the redolent air. There was in it a quality of benign provenience – a quality that was particular, Dr. Swarthmore thought, to nights at the end of summer.

He alighted finally in the driveway of a frame farmhouse. He climbed the porch. No one answered his knock. Frowning, he opened the door and entered the darkness of the hall. A line of unsteady yellow light showed under the door at the end of the hall. Dr. Swarthmore groped his way to the door and went in.

The light was dim and strangely hectic; it flickered rapidly upon the walls and furnishings of the room. A wick needed trimming. Dr. Swarthmore saw a disorderly yellowish something that was heaped up against the opposite wall like soiled laundry piled in a sink. Then his eyes sorted things out – he was staring at the invalid. The man's wife and a pair of adolescent daughters were ranged on their knees along the foot of the iron bed, murmurously but strenuously at prayer.

It occurred to Dr. Swarthmore that his entrance upon this scene had perhaps been too abrupt, and that it might be tactful to withdraw himself for the time being. On the other hand, he was drawn by the aspect of the figure on the bed. The bedclothes were exploded as if the body were a bomb that had been tossed among them, and the body itself lay all but naked on the bare disordered sheets. Dr. Swarthmore was astonished by its emaciation: bovine hips, ribs like a stove grate. The yellow skin stretched tautly under the ribs was like cracked parchment. The rapid oscillations of the light seemed to displace the figure minutely to the left, the right, the left again; and this appearance of shuttle-like motion caused the Doctor's gaze to lose its focus.

Abruptly the light was still. The body was motionless. Dr. Swarthmore, starting slightly, realized that the women had turned their heads to look at him. He got down heavily on to his knees beside the bed, placed his hat on the floor and bowed his head. After a minute or two he rolled his eyes up and obtained a peripheral view of the figure on the bed. The body was vehemently rigid: the spine was bowed by a tension so violent that the apprehension of it set the Doctor's teeth on edge. An intense heat radiated from the bed. Dr. Swarthmore wished that he could take off his coat. He imagined that he saw the body glow – glow like hot iron – and for an instant he believed that it was the true source of the light in the room. The idea made him bring his gaze up. The women were silent now but still on their knees; only their faces showed between the slender bars of the bedframe. The row of faces wavered and bobbed, receded minutely into shadow and eased into the light again. The faces were abstracted, incurious, comatose. A wedge of shadow lay against each nose. The opposite cheek was rounded against the shadows behind it like the limb of the moon.

The hours passed. The light contracted and the room grew cavernous. The walls became indistinct and the ceiling withdrew into shadow. What enforced this withdrawal (Dr. Swarthmore imagined) was the steady diffusion of time into the room: time discharged, as gas is discharged from a cylinder, by the object on the bed – the sublimation of its impacted years. The Doctor shifted his weight from knee to knee and thought about the cigars inside his coat.

Toward midnight the dying man stirred. He rose stiffly amid the hot sheets. He cried aloud that he looked beyond the gates of death and saw –

Then fell back dead. His cry seemed to have dinted the air, to have made a shape in it. The wife and the daughters rushed the bed. Dr. Swarthmore stayed on his knees, staring. He felt gingerly and remote. He had no more aptitude for motion than a stump has. With his vision oppressed by some sudden viscosity in the air, or in the fluid of his eyes, he watched uncomprehendingly as the women stripped the sheets – they rolled the corpse from side to side in order to do it – and gathered them into a ball. The younger girl carried the bundle out of the room at arm's length, holding the smallest possible area of fabric between thumb and forefinger. Her sister pulled the curtains aside and opened the windows. Their mother fiddled with a paraffin lamp on the dresser beside the bed. The room brightened. Dr. Swarthmore blinked.

The younger girl returned, wiping her hands on her skirt, and the three women herded together in the middle of the room. They made various small and, as it seemed, preparatory movements, putting out a foot, drawing it back, pushing at their sleeves. Dr. Swarthmore was visited by the grotesque idea that they were about to break into a buck-and-wing. Instead, with a howl that made his scalp jump, they flung themselves onto the bed, where they draped the corpse in their long, disordered hair.

A strange listlessness had come upon Dr. Swarthmore. He seemed to float like a log on the rising flood of the women's grief. As that grief filled up the room, it displaced him out of it. He rose and went from the place, past the dead man's keening family, then out the front door and past his own horse and trap in the drive. He walked like a man in a dream. His thoughts were wordless, formless, slow and black. At some point he had ignited a cigar; its smoke, rising in measured puffs in the motionless air, expressed the shape and tempo of his mood.

He had no sense of his surroundings until, by degrees, he became aware of the silence of the night. This silence was profound. As he listened, expecting some qualification of the silence – a random cricket, a dog chanting at the moon – the silence, or his apprehension of it, instead grew more complete. The silence seemed to stratify, to accumulate in layers, interring him as a fossil shell is interred in beds of limestone. And now he heard, from a great distance, or from the spiralled chamber of his own inner ear, a murmur like the unending murmur of the sea.

He looked up sharply and saw that he was on a narrow country road. Fields of stubble stretched away to the left and the right. No light showed anywhere. Overhead was sheet of dully luminous cloud, very low, set like an iron lid on the rim of the horizon.

Dr. Swarthmore accepted this rudimentary prospect at a glance. Yet between the glance and the acceptance lay an instant in which the prospect looked alien and terrible, dangerous to himself. It was as if he had surprised it by raising his eyes so quickly. The Doctor frowned. Then he inclined his head and prepared to resume his walk.

He took a step, perhaps two steps. A circle of sudden light splashed the dust at his feet. Startled, he threw his head back. A deep circular breach had opened in the clouds. Beyond this cavity rode the full moon, as hard and as bright as a dollar. Its chilly light, preternaturally clear and strong, dropped through the chasm in a brilliant shaft that glazed the encircling clouds with glory.

The Doctor had scarcely apprehended this display when something began to descend on the fall of light. It was a form, a being – a being as insubstantial as the light itself. Dr. Swarthmore did not doubt his senses. He saw what he saw. But he was astonished all the same.

The creature slid effortlessly down its moonbeam and at last stood upon the road directly before the Doctor. Its hands were upheld in a benedictory gesture. It had the shape of a man, more or less, but the details of this shape, especially of the face, were obscured by moonlight or by the creature's own interior luminosity – if the distinction could be made. The head was circled by tonguelets of cold fire.

The Being spoke; or rather Dr. Swarthmore felt within his mind the intrusion of its projected thought, as sometimes we hear voices without word or tongue as a cry in our sleep or a murmur out of the forest – voices that in no degree modify the external silence, but seem instead to be agents of that silence.

The Being told Dr. Swarthmore to open his mind and heart, for he was to receive great truths.

There was a longish pause. Dr. Swarthmore was at a loss. As he pondered a response he put his hand into his coat, took out two cigars and absently extended the hand that held them toward the Being – then realized what he was doing, returned one cigar to his pocket and lit the other. The Doctor smoked diligently for a while, eager to avoid the Being's gaze, if it had one. Finally he opened his mouth to say something pleasant and noncommittal, but before he could speak his mind was filled with an apprehension of the universal mechanism – an apparatus that had worlds and suns for cogs and wheels, the Milky Way for a flywheel; and somewhere within it, obscurely and uncertainly placed, God for a governor. Dr. Swarthmore dropped his cigar. He was so impressed by this machine that some time passed before he noticed a puzzling circumstance: it wasn't going.

The Being spoke again. It explained that this was the day – the very hour and moment, in fact – of the autumnal equinox: a moment in which the heavens sustained a perfect balance, in which the proportion of light was precisely equal to the share of darkness, an instant of stasis before the stars renewed their motions, before life and death resumed. Only during moments of this kind could the temporal sphere receive the presence of intemporal Beings, or Beings that did not partake of time. Although the moment could have no duration (just as a point in space could not possess extension), the Being had the power to hold off time for a certain term.

Dr. Swarthmore frowned, for he was unhappy with the idea that time could be suspended for a time. But the very paradoxicalness of the idea convinced him, after a minute's reflection, that he was indeed on the threshold of a potent mystery.

As he registered this conviction, the Being stirred within its beam of moonshine and spoke of the season about to begin: the season of decay, of universal katabolism, the suzerainty of night and death. The Being enlarged upon the horrors of the tomb, upon the inexorable labour of worms and things that creep, upon the patience of the skull behind its mask of flesh. To all of these things did the flesh incline.

The Doctor lit and drew energetically on a fresh cigar. But despite its fumatory virtue a corrupted breath blew against his face; blew ever more insistently, until it seemed that he could taste it.

Behold, said the Being, and Dr. Swarthmore cautiously lowered his cigar. Behold, the sun is renewed, the year swings back toward stasis. And the Doctor beheld mountains of prismatic ice, the firmament hung with draperies of imperial light. He stood of an instant upon a level sheet of ice – white-blue ice upon a blue-black sea – and saw the stars in grand rotation; and he was himself the axle of that tremendous wheel. The cold was absolute. The Doctor stood within it – or it within him – and the air sang like crystal pinged with a fingernail.

But all too soon, murmured the Herald of God (and the illumined figure inclined itself, in a rather disagreeably intimate way, toward the Doctor's ear), flux and disorder have their turn again.

And now the Being caused Dr. Swarthmore to see phantoms or images of the things that live and spawn upon the earth. He saw chitinous monsters with eyes like rubber nubs on sticks swarm and chitter upon a stinking tidal flat, then stepped backwards, in a reflex of disgust, into a hummocked field of ragged and poisonous-looking weeds. There was a sweet, nauseous odour of spermy sap, a booming of insects' wings. A herd of grunting quadrupeds shuffled past, filling the

Doctor's prospect with the spectacle of their richly spouting fundaments. He spun away, gulping compulsively, only to see a shuddering heap of frogs – thousands of frogs – engaged helter-skelter in mass copulation. The welter of frogs immediately became a pair of ardent lovers, who shrieked and tore at one another's flesh, and tumbled witlessly one over the other in their distraction.

The lovers became a pair of smooth pale serpents wrapped together in the moonlit dust at Dr. Swarthmore's feet, where they flopped awkwardly and bit one another about the head. The Being stepped forward and ground them with its shining foot. A shout filled heaven and earth.

The Being seized Dr. Swarthmore's wrist in a grip that was as cool and as light as freshly powdered snow, yet irresistible, and drew him into the shaft of moonlight. They rose upon the shaft, and Dr. Swarthmore felt a slight giddiness, as if he were riding in a swiftly ascendant elevator. He had been in an elevator once, in Indianapolis, and so it was that the analogy occurred to him.

The Herald of God brought Dr. Swarthmore to a high and barren place where the wind tore at his eyes and made him blink. The moon, so bright that it showed no features, caused the boulders to throw huge, misshapen shadows. The Being made a gesture that bade the Doctor to look down.

Below them lay a dark plain scattered to the horizon with clusters of coruscating lights. At first Dr. Swarthmore supposed that they were the remains of fires – the leaf fires of an autumn evening – and that they were neither large nor far away. But after a minute's study he realized that they were the lights of cities and understood that he looked upon the entire world.

The Being's radiant form wavered, and the nearest collection of lights swam up toward them, until Dr. Swarthmore could see its every detail. It was Indianapolis. It was the morning, nacreous, calm and cold, of the twenty-first day of March in the year nineteen hundred and one, and Jesus Christ had returned to the earth. He emerged from Union Station in the guise of a drummer, wearing a checked suit and lugging a sample case – which Dr. Swarthmore knew, by some mysterious agency, was full of shoes, right foot only.

Dr. Swarthmore saw Jesus pause at the mouth of an alley where two rough-looking men sat on their hunkers and threw dice against the wall. He heard him speak – only a few words – and saw the men pocket those dice, and rise up and follow him.

He saw the living Christ approach a young drugstore idler, a youth addicted to racy slang and flashy neckties, and to smoking cigarettes with a dissipated smirk. Jesus spoke: the lounger threw his cigarette away; his eyes flashed with a clean and manly light – and he followed him.

The Son of Man came abreast of the louvred doors of a saloon. From behind the doors came piano music, brutish laughter, the rattle of glassware. He went inside. The piano produced a discord. The laughter faded. Jesus came forth again, and after an interval the patrons of the place filed out behind him, dumb, sheepish and blinking – but with a firm set to their shoulders, and with the light of the Lord in their eyes.

The Lamb of God entered a house of prostitution. His retinue waited on the sidewalk. There was heard a universal creaking of bedsprings, a Babel of wondering voices. Jesus descended to the pavement. Down the steps behind him came a dozen men, some of whom were still fastening their trouser buttons; and among them, with their kimonos held tightly shut at throat and bosom, came the women of the place. One of these nightingales happened to brush the arm of her escort, whereupon they hastily stepped apart.

So Jesus went about the city, smiting wickedness from the hearts of men. The city fell into step behind him, a numberless, enraptured host, with its thousands of eyes glued to his back as he led it along.

Dr. Swarthmore found himself an atom of this multitude. The crowd shuffled along docilely, sending up a good-natured murmur – the way a crowd might sound upon leaving the ball park after a well-played game. Jesus led it through the commercial district and out into the residential suburbs. The day was tolerably warm, for March. A light wind brought a smell of dampness and chilly earth from the lawns. The pavement was dotted with puddles, and Dr. Swarthmore walked with his head down, picking his steps, since his shoes tended to admit water between the soles and the uppers – a circumstance that led him to facetious thoughts about Jesus's sample case and its contents.

The Doctor became so absorbed in stepping around and over puddles that he failed to take in a rumour that was passing back through the crowd – failed as well to notice the excitement that arose wherever the rumour touched. The people behind the Doctor began to push and jostle him along, forcing him at last to stumble through quite a deepish puddle. Before he could remonstrate, they had elbowed him to one side and rushed on. He looked ruefully at his shoes.

A swarming, hive-like murmur was rising behind him. The Doctor turned, frowning.

Five yards of clear ground stood between Dr. Swarthmore and the next instalment of crowd. He had time enough in which to hear and to comprehend the roar of that mob – Jesus was leading them to the cemetery! He was going to raise a man from the dead!

Then Dr. Swarthmore was lifted bodily by the stampede, which went headlong for twenty yards, caught its feet on the Doctor and went down in a pile, picked itself up and swept forward again. In this manner – falling all over itself – the multitude arrived at the cemetery, annihilated the gate and a quarter-mile of green picket fence and swarmed up the slope after the sauntering figure of Jesus. Half of its members came to grief against the headstones and monuments, like mayflies drifting a windowsill.

Jesus gained the top of the slope. He turned and lifted his

hands. Silence fell like a stone. Dr. Swarthmore, his hat askew and his collar sprung, apprehended no sound but that of his own and his neighbours' weary and convulsive breathing. It was hot in that herd. The Doctor shucked his coat, never taking his eyes from the jaunty figure outlined upon a sky that was bright and flawlessly blue, the medium or habitation of God.

Jesus too took off his coat, then draped it, with humorous nonchalance, over a handy gravestone. There was tittering in the multitude, which Jesus acknowledged with a wink. He approached a handsome limestone vault and walked once around it as he rolled up his shirtsleeves, exposing a pair of comely and athletic forearms. Then, with a mighty heave, he threw off the lid. A little appreciative whistling and clapping from the multitude. Jesus shrugged self-deprecatingly and walked slowly around the vault again, rubbing his chin. Suddenly he reached in with both arms and wrestled out the coffin. Strong applause from the multitude. Jesus waved it away and turned to prop the coffin upright against the vault. He took a screwdriver from his hip pocket and went to work on the lid. The multitude shuffled closer.

The lid sprang off. In that instant a light wind, a mere catspaw, passed over the hillside, bringing down with it a smell so forceful, so vile, so detestable in its associations that the multitude recoiled by sheer protoplasmal instinct, like a sea-jelly on a tidal rock. Then it looked at what was in the coffin. A man who stood beside Dr. Swarthmore rolled up his eyes and slid bonelessly to the ground.

Dr. Swarthmore frowned. The contents of the coffin as such disturbed him less than the idea that those contents were about to be refurbished. Suppose, he thought, lighting a cigar to subdue the air a little, suppose that some day he met this man – how would he feel about that? Wouldn't the smell of that smell linger about him always?

The multitude, meanwhile, was sorry that it had come. A complicated murmuring, at once indignant, beseechful and appalled, boiled off its surface like a vapour. No one wanted to look. They all looked.

'That's just about enough, God damn it,' someone shouted finally. 'Fix him up and get him out of there.' 'That's right!' 'Let's go!' 'Come *on*!' cried the multitude – and a chastened and plaintive multitude it was now, too. But Jesus did nothing.

Finally he spoke. 'I wanted you to have a good long look,' he said mildly. He lifted a hand to his mouth, pursed his lips and blew a kiss into the coffin. When he stepped back again the coffin was – empty.

Silence from the multitude. Then a gasp that used up the air for half a mile around.

'Well, I'm jiggered!' a voice behind Dr. Swarthmore said.

'And I'm a Dutchman,' replied another voice. 'But you know, it's not exactly what we were led to expect, is it?'

'It's not even close,' said the first voice. Then, dolefully: 'To tell the truth, if that fellow up there wasn't who he is, I'd say we've been sold a bill of goods.'

'I don't care *who* he is.' A third, more pungent voice joined the other two. 'We've been sold, all right. The question is, what do we do about it?'

Other voices in Dr. Swarthmore's neighbourhood were addressing the same question. The multitude had clotted into a thousand hotly eloquent little groups of three or four or five. It was, at a glance, as if the multitude had determined suddenly to dispute within itself the several sides of a difficult issue. In fact – as Dr. Swarthmore, who did not participate in any of the talk, was reasonably quick to realize – there was no dispute: the multitude was simply making clear to itself a proper sense of the imposition it had suffered. The clots rapidly broke up; the multitude, its homogeneity restored, milled about at random for a minute or two. Then, in a mysterious community of reflex, and with cries of 'Sold! Sold!', it rushed the slope.

Jesus sat on the edge of the vault, negligently swinging his legs. When the mob was almost upon him, he raised one hand, hid a yawn with the other, and dropped lightly to the ground. The multitude shrank back – for in his manner there was, after all, something transcendental and grand.

'Sure you've been sold,' said Jesus, cocking his thumbs in his vest. 'Wasn't what you came for, was it? But on the level, now, aren't you relieved it turned out this way? Sure you are! Suppose I'd set that ruin going – and I could have, if I'd wanted to –' and again Jesus winked at the multitude '– wouldn't you have felt pretty funny about that? *Sure* you would have. And say,' he added, with an air of humorous afterthought, 'how do you think *he* would have liked it, coming around in front of the whole aggregated population of Indianapolis with hardly a scrap on him? But the way it turned out, I'd say I've done a good turn for all concerned. Well, haven't I? Haven't I now? Come on, don't be bashful. Haven't I? *Sure* I have!'

The multitude thought it over. Its members found themselves grinning obliquely at one another. Eyeball met eyeball in mutual sheepishness. A woman giggled. A farmer slapped his thigh.

Then the multitude laughed. The laughter rolled back through the crowd and forward again, rank upon rank, wave upon wave. Sturdy American multitude that it was, it knew how to take a joke, though the joke was at its own expense. Even Dr. Swarthmore felt a smirk worry its way out of his beard. A man who stood near him, a city dude whose lapels were smeared with billiard chalk, turned and clapped him on the back.

'Say, there, granpa,' the stranger cried. 'That was a hell of a show – am I right?' Dr. Swarthmore nodded gravely, and when he had put his coat on again he offered the other a cigar. The multitude was spreading itself out, but it showed no inclination to go home. Absently, through a pleasant befuddlement, Dr. Swarthmore was aware that couples were passing in amorous promenade among the headstones and willows, that family groups were settling themselves on the grass. Laughter and conversation carried from every side on the benevolent, dim and somewhat muffling air. The dude swung his gaze around idly, prodded the turf with his stick. Dr. Swarthmore rocked on his heels, with his hands clasped behind his back, and enjoyed his cigar.

A whisk of colour, like a flag or a signal, caught the corner of his eye. A few feet away a woman was flapping the creases out of a checkered tablecloth. As the cloth settled to the ground it discovered the approach of a pair of adolescent girls, one on each side of an enormous picnic hamper. With no change in his benign but woolly state of mind, Dr. Swarthmore recognized the wife and daughters of the man he had lately attended on his deathbed. Though that had been in September. Now it was March. While the Doctor tried to imagine what the Celestial Being had done with the intervening months, the daughters, looking plumper than they had looked the other time, sat down on the cloth and began to empty the hamper of its cargo of cold meats, bottled pickles and preserves.

The dude watched this operation with a narrow gaze. A little breast of chicken, he said, would be just the thing right now. Dr. Swarthmore agreed: he was a touch hungry himself. His new acquaintance laughed and clapped him on the back again, then strolled over to join the picnickers, lifted his hat, leered.

And when the man leered, showing a row of neat white teeth, Dr. Swarthmore's brain burned suddenly with an image of the coffin and its contents, and his heart rolled into his stomach. His gaze travelled fearfully over the heads of the picnickers (the dude wrestled with the lid of a pickle jar, the daughters giggled) and up the hill behind them. The coffin stood empty, spic and span. And now the Doctor's relief and gratitude came in a flood, lifting his gaze beyond the hill and its monuments to the blue unbounded sky. To look at this sky was to rise into it. Dr. Swarthmore rose, buoyed by a spirit as pure and untroubled – as limpid – as the crystalline heaven itself.

Again Dr. Swarthmore stood beside the Herald of God, which so disposed its airy microscope that the Doctor apprehended the entire globe. This vision was so terrific, so complete, that the Doctor was unable to distinguish himself from it. He both saw and was all that he saw. He saw the components of the world, the trillion trillion trillion of them, not only severally and in themselves but also in all of the complexity of their relations with one another, and he himself participated in this complexity, encompassed it, embodied it. Dr. Swarthmore saw, and was, everything that is the case.

Presently, however, separation came. The Doctor was precipitated out of his own universalization as a crystal is precipitated out of a solution of salts. He was, once more, nothing more than himself, and his hands were astonished to feel the bulk and the elasticity of his flesh (and the corrugation of his nested cigars) through the cloth of his coat.

And now, far, far below him, a single object moved to and fro upon the earth, and all the cities sang. This object was the Christ.

For a time his progress was unopposed. But presently the princes and suzerains of the earth grew jealous of the upstart. They conspired to destroy him, and to this end they put into motion, irretrievably, their machineries of war. Dr. Swarthmore was shown a confusing *montage* of martial images: British warships standing out to sea; Prussian uhlans galloping across the Baltic dunes; the united Catholic armies of France, Austria and Italy bending the knee before the Pope – while a sea of Russian infantry did the same under the blessings of the metropolitans of Moscow and St. Petersburg. The Christ's response was to organize an army of his own – a legion of the righteous, which he arrayed provocatively upon a level plain. From every corner of the world the secular armies swarmed down upon this mettlesome little band. The sun retired behind the smoke of cities, nations, empires. The innocent fell without number. Again and again Dr.

Swarthmore winced behind his cigar. But in the end Christ was master of the world.

Certain renovations were made, justifying the prophet: 'Every valley shall be filled, and every mountain and hill shall be brought low; and the crooked shall be made straight, and the rough ways shall be made smooth; and all flesh shall see the salvation of God.'

Jesus checked the ancient motions of the universe and placed the world out of time, so that his kingdom would endure forever.

Now Dr. Swarthmore walked the streets of the perdurable City of God, the reality whose shadow is the world. He had passed from time into eternity, and he was properly impressed. The sun, nailed to the zenith, bathed the buildings of the city in a shadowless glare. The buildings themselves were vast, blank and silent. The Doctor met no one. Everything he saw – he saw only architecture – was fixed in a profound immobility.

Nevertheless, he approached every corner in the conviction that he had only to turn it to discover movement and life. The people of this city, he was certain, would be tall and almost translucently pale, wrapped in stately togas that fell about their feet like marble drapery. They would be ageless, deathless. He would see wisdom and certitude stamped on every pallid brow.

The Doctor wondered where he had gotten these ideas. In any case, every corner was a disappointment, and all of the streets were silent and empty.

Dr. Swarthmore walked in the changeless light, walked endlessly and without fatigue. Every block of buildings was the same as every other block. These enormous volumes suggested nothing, led to nothing. Yet he had a sense of destination – a conviction that he was, in fact, going somewhere.

There was more to this than intuition. Dr. Swarthmore had observed that the traverse streets were laid out not in straight lines but in enormously extended curves. As the streets succeeded one another, the curvature became more apparent and the blocks on the curve became shorter. Yet the change was so gradual that Dr. Swarthmore was obliged to look down hundreds or thousands of streets before he could make up his mind about them. Finally, he ventured two conclusions: first, that the pattern of streets was at once radial and concentric, like a spider's web (and in this respect the City of God had an affinity with Indianapolis); second, that he was following one of the radials to its point of intersection with all of the other radials.

No doubt the extension of the radial streets was infinite – how could the City of God be circumscribed? But the meeting of the radials would be a point of utter finitude, a finality most final. It goes without saying that Dr. Swarthmore was curious to see what form this finality would take.

Fortunately his curiosity was willing to bide its time. The illusory, or subjective, point of convergence at the end of the vista retreated steadily before his advance; it was, in effect, a moving screen for the *real* point of convergence that necessarily lay beyond. The vista would in fact have to open before it closed. Dr. Swarthmore did not relish this paradox. Nor did he relish the utter absence, at the end of the vista, of the irresolution that is a normal function of distance – or, more precisely, a function of the scattering of light by the air that stands between the eye and its object. The buildings nearest the vanishing point, though they were so far away that he had to screw up his eyes in order to see them, were defined in the same tones and displayed the same clarity of outline as the buildings immediately at hand. The Doctor had the disagreeable sensation that he was constantly about to walk into a painted backdrop. What he needed was something that he could interpose between himself and the view. His cigar did the trick. Puffing hard, he sustained a body of smoke and used it to establish a system of perspective in which the more distant buildings were, indeed, manifestly more distant. The Doctor was pleased with his ingenuity, and the pleasure persisted even when he became too winded to raise more smoke.

Abruptly the tip of the street's interminable wedge was nipped away. The prospect confirmed its finitude. A building stood in the gap, and as the gap grew wider with his approach the Doctor saw that the building's single dome was lifted far above every other dome and tower in the city. He had no doubt that this stupendous building was the repository of whatever revelation awaited him.

The street opened finally into a vast circular plaza whose curve showed the Doctor the mouths of a thousand other streets; the streets were like rivers that emptied into a tideless sea. In the centre of the plaza, with a face toward each of the streets, and in each face a door, stood the cyclopean polygonal base of a dome far more huge than Dr. Swarthmore had ever imagined a dome could be. He had to throw his head back as far as it would go in order to see the top of the dome. Yet it was plain, given the enormous circumference of the plaza, that the building was still at a great distance from where he stood.

It was in Dr. Swarthmore's nature to take things as he found them. Even so, as he started across the plaza he was seized by a sense of the recklessness of the enterprise. He felt as if he were setting out upon the open sea in a dinghy. The Doctor was obliged to remind himself that when one has spent three round score of years in the world one is, in a sense, prepared for any-thing, since no new thing can then be wholly new. The plaza was vast, and flat, and featureless; but these were adjectives that applied with nearly equal force to north-central Indiana. And so his hesitation passed in a moment.

It might have lasted longer, though, had he known how truly vast the plaza was. He walked interminably; nevertheless, although the building filled his entire field of vision, it grew no nearer. Once he turned and looked back. He was astonished to see that the roofs of the buildings on the rim of the plaza made a line not half a degree above the horizon. He was obliged to revise, exponentially, his idea of the hugeness of the building that stood before him. From this point he was subject to a mild but persistent discomfort, analogous to the sensations of a man seated before a fire: the openness of the plaza chilled his back; the overbearing mass of the building made his face feel stifled. He began as well to feel self-conscious about his motility in the face of the perfect stasis of everything outside himself. The sun, conventionally an agent of change, was fixed to the dead perpendicular. It distributed its light impartially over the whole blank surface of the dome and denied to Dr. Swarthmore the companionship of his shadow. With every step he felt a growing obligation to apologize for his animateness to the plaza, the dome and the motionless sun.

At last, unelated, he climbed the porch of the innermost tabernacle of the City of God. The great doors – brazen, unadorned – stood open, but as he came forward to enter them he felt an obscure twinge of caution. Not fear, but a kind of skepticism or dubiety. He stopped on the threshold and peered into the vastness and dimness within, then cocked his head and strained to sift some morsel of sound from the gigantic silence.

Finally he straightened himself up, coughed into his hand, and went inside. Absolute darkness swallowed him up. He walked blindly along a level corridor, and he came to wonder if he might not walk along it forever. At intervals, when he lit his cigars, he saw that the corridor was as featureless as a drainpipe. This corridor, he was certain, was in effect an extension of the street that had led him to the plaza. Presumably there were thousands of identical corridors, all converging on a central point. Dr. Swarthmore was becoming resentful of the insistent impulsiveness of the arrangement. *He* had not solicited this expedition. He trusted that it was worth his while.

Suddenly the corridor opened and he was in a lofty rotunda. The blank interior of the dome arched hundreds – thousands – of feet above his head. A shaft of chilly moonlight fell through an opening in the apex of the dome to scour acres of marble floor. The shaft was so dense that it baffled the sight.

He entered this stupendous hall a step at a time. He listened.

As he listened he became afraid. The silence made him afraid. The hair rose implacably all over his body. The silence of the streets and the plaza was bedlam to it. It was silence with mass, silence as a presence. It was the silence at the end of the world.

And yet, in some cool, cool recess of his soul, he felt superior to the place, skeptical of it, so that even as fear put hands on him he could not abstain from diminishing the hall, in his own mind, by deciding that it reminded him of the central concourse of Union Station in Indianapolis. It was larger, maybe – he didn't have a tape measure with him – but the same kind of thing. And this comparison, whether he had willed it or whether it was the reflex of an indestructibly commonplace mind, made him smile in his beard.

Dr. Swarthmore lit a cigar. It did not surprise him to discover that this cigar was his last. He was willing to believe that the dimensions of the City of God had been determined by the number of cigars he had carried with him at the start and by the probable (or predestined) frequency of his urge to smoke one.

The cigar encouraged him to step deeper into the vastness of the hall, to let his shoes ring boldly on the pavement. He approached the column of moonlight and saw within it, elevated on a narrow plinth, the semblance or apparition of a human figure. The moonlight obscured rather than revealed, but it was certain that the figure stood perfectly and narrowly upright, with no movement or extension of its limbs. As Dr. Swarthmore came forward, the figure became momentarily more narrow still, then grew wider again. The Doctor paused just at the margin of the moonlight to puzzle the matter out. Evidently the figure was turning on its base. It was in a state of slow but incessant rotation, in which it endlessly swept with its gaze the whole uncircumferentiated circle of the City of God; a circle that its gaze created or sustained. The Doctor stepped into the moonlight, shuddering slightly at what seemed to be the touch of it on his shoulders.

The figure turned, disclosing its face. Dr. Swarthmore dropped his cigar. He had seen that face – or rather that face-lessness – before. In the next moment he began to rise on the beam of moonshine, and when he again found himself standing on the country road in Indiana – the clouds were restored, the moon was gone – he retained the knowledge that the dead figure would turn and turn in that monstrous hall, unseen and unseeing, down through eternity. That knowledge and also the knowledge, even harder to digest than the other, that he had indeed been sold.

The Sermon

Alexander Hamilton Blount, a student at Dr. Swarthmore's college, owned a stake-sided delivery wagon and an angular, graceless horse that looked, even when it moved, as if it had been put together – by a savage, perhaps, or a child – out of dead sticks. The same description applied to Blount himself, though he did not move as much as the horse did.

Every Tuesday, Thursday and Saturday morning, at the crack of dawn, Blount drove his rig out of the shed behind his boarding house. The bed of the wagon bulked irregularly under a grey tarpaulin. Discovered by the horizontal sun, wagon and horse and man together composed an entity that seemed provisional and indeterminate, the product of an impulse not yet conscious of an end. The college's History Department, kept awake all night by a toothache, glanced out of his bedroom window in time to look down upon Blount, horse and mysteriously burdened wagon as they passed eastward along Main Street with their composite shadow drawn out behind them like the dwindling province of night itself, which they might have been dragging off to the village dump. The History Department stepped back into the room. He was troubled by an image of something that had just been turned out into the light, something stiff and uncouth but pregnant with futurity, like an artifact dug out of a tumulus. Then his toothache put its knife into him and he fell groaning across the bed.

On another morning, the proprietor of the hardware store on the edge of town stood before his establishment and unpacked a crate that had just arrived from the station. He was about to enter the store with an armload of long-handled shovels when Blount's wagon appeared jerkily from behind the building on the corner, crossed the head of the street and disappeared behind the building on the opposite corner. The hardware man thought of a tin duck in a shooting gallery. Then he thought of a cast-iron mechanical bank into which no one had as yet put any money. Then he stepped forward and put the handles of those shovels right through the bevelled glass of the door.

Blount, primly erect on the worn board seat, drove his wagon out of the village and into the countryside, his gaze fitted to the ruts in the strip of dust that vanished endlessly between the horse's ears. Eventually he turned in at one or another of the farms along the road, twitched the reins – the horse, once it had stopped, contrived to look as if it had been assembled where it stood – and climbed down. He put his hand under the seat and pulled out a large cardboard suitcase with A.H. BLOUNT stencilled on it.

As Blount crossed the yard to the door, with the chickens pecking at his shoes, he accomplished a metamorphosis. His eyes, the colour of a galvanized bucket, fired abruptly with a cheerful twinkle. His bloodless lips withdrew from teeth that were like kernels of milky young corn, and a pair of rosy dimples dinted his cheeks, which a moment ago had seemed meagre and waxen. His body relinquished its angles and became supple. His step became brisk, his bearing cheerfully assertive. Yet even as he came forward he seemed visibly to hold back, presenting in this way an attractive picture of brashness tempered by diffidence. Modifying all of these qualities, inimical to none of them, an air of Sunday-school religiosity draped his stripling's shoulders like an impalpable gauze.

But this creature, when complete, was less an identity than a category of possible identities. What Blount was, finally, was up to the person who opened the door. The farmer's wife confronted the dimples, the callowness, the remote but incontrovertible fragrance of religion. But her husband got a virile handshake and a broad plowboy grin. Or some other combination or shading of qualities was arranged.

Once he had been specified by the person in the doorway, Blount cast out his line of talk and reeled himself into the house after it – a patter of kitchen or barnyard gossip that led to a moment in which it was the most natural and graceful thing in the world that he should open his cardboard suitcase and produce something pertinent to the conversation: a can of stove enamel, a box of Rough on Rats, a set of suspenders, a specific for hog cholera; or perhaps a brochure, illustrated with steel engravings, that described the Vesuvius line of phonographs – it was several of these phonographs, with some sewing machines, cream separators and other bulky stock, that he kept under the tarpaulin in the wagon.

When Blount left the house – and he left, inevitably, with less in his suitcase than was in it when he came – he relapsed by degrees into his former rigidity, which was complete by the time he regained his seat in the wagon and drove away.

In this way Blount paid his fees at the college and kept himself at Mrs. Whelan's boarding house. More than kept himself: he had accumulated capital. Idle capital, sewn into his mattress. It may have bothered him that it was idle.

Apart from visiting the farms, Blount's only pastime was his religion. He was nineteen years old, and he had read the Bible from front to back nineteen times. This was coincidence. He read the Bible without prejudice, applying the same stony attention as he gave to the Gospels to Nahum, Habakkuk, Zephaniah, the dedicatory epistle to King James and the coloured endpaper maps of the Holy Land. He never missed a love feast or a prayer meeting. He was a perfect teetotaller and did not use tobacco. He never walked under the trees with any of the village sirens. Nor did he practice self-abuse. He could be heard through the flimsy walls of his room as he prayed monotonously to his God.

Finally Providence offered this seminarian an opportunity to put his two activities to mutual service. No contradiction there: God and Mammon had shaken hands over his cradle.

Blount's opportunity was disclosed to him on a Sunday morning in mid-October. Blount sat on a window aisle. Outside it was windy: clouds covered and uncovered the sun, and the church by turns swelled with light, dwindled into dimness again. When the sun came out, its light fell upon Blount through a hundred rhombic panes of richly coloured glass. The pattern of green and orange light broke out upon him instantaneously, as if his skin had blossomed in a cheerful motley of decay. But then the light went out of the window again, and as it went Blount's figure condensed, drew itself together, ordered itself. The interior of the church became smaller and smaller, the very air compact, and hard, and perfectly still; was on the verge of setting that way forever – when, with epiphanic suddenness, the light returned, broke Blount to bits, and made the air swell.

Dr. Swarthmore ascended his pulpit.

'Romans ten twenty,' said the Doctor. ' "I was found of them that sought me not; I was made manifest unto them that asked not after me.' "

Dr. Swarthmore read this text in a hasty monotone, and with his head so deeply inclined that he seemed to be addressing someone crouched under the lectern. But now he looked up, blinked.

'I have seen the ocean just once in my life.' The Doctor's voice was now informed by a remote howling or baying quality, as of a pack of hounds heard from three ridges away. 'It was years ago, the only time I've ever been so far from Indiana. The ocean is a marvellous work – but I won't describe it to you. Instead, I'll tell you what the ocean did to me.

'There is some necessary preamble. I must tell you that when I made this journey I had been a minister of the living gospel for a good many years, and yet that gospel did not live for *me*. I had entered the ministry for no better reason than that it was the custom in my family to enter it. All of my ancestors had assumed the cloth. I did not feel strongly enough about the matter to reject an example that had become, by sheer repetition, a species of necessity. And so I went through seminary, ordination and fifteen years of pastorship without batting an eye, though in my heart I was a perfect infidel.

'Not that I knew it. From my father I had received the idea of a God so extreme in his majesty, so vastly superior to his creatures, that it was clearly impossible for me to have anything to do with him. In seminary my companions told me of their experiences of a personal God who had touched and transmuted their souls. I listened and said nothing, but I told myself that they lied. How these insects diminish God, thought I, in supposing that he would meddle with their paltriness! For my own part, I had made a covenant with God: if he would leave me undisturbed in my insecthood, I would not tamper with his majesty. Well and good. Fifteen years later, when I packed my bags and went off to enjoy what I considered to be a well-deserved holiday, nothing had happened to trouble this adamantine egoism of mine, this criminal neutrality of conscience.

'I arrived at my seaside hotel after dark, stepping almost directly from the enclosed omnibus that had brought me from the station into the quiet and well-ordered lobby of the inn. Yet in crossing that narrow span of ground I had time in which to feel that I had come to the edge of the world. Here were noise, wind, cold, damp – like so many murderous vagabonds, falling upon me as I stepped from the carriage. Instead of the decent fixity of earth that had lain before me, in any direction I faced, all of my landlocked life, the darkness concealed a bowelless anarchy, a raw tumultuous emptiness upon whose seething rim I had inconsiderately placed myself. The ocean, which I had not yet seen, was a cancer gnawing the margins of the ordered sphere. All that night I heard the commotion of the surf, and woke repeatedly from dreams of falling into the void. Again and again I hugged the bolster, to save my life.

'But the morning was bright and fine, and I felt like a fool. From my window the ocean looked docile and even cheerful. I watched the waves pile into sheaves of foam as they closed upon the sand and chided myself, in a good-natured way, for failing to remember that the ocean is as much a part of God's dominion as is Indiana – which, in its horizontalness at least, the ocean somewhat resembled.

'Friends, what a coward bully is our human nature. As soon as we lose our fear we begin to swagger. We belittle – we abuse – the source of our recent dread. As soon as I had decided that the ocean did not deserve my terror I began to wonder if it merited my respect. To tell the truth, it was just a trifle boring – all that water. But I had travelled a thousand miles to see it, and I hated to think that I had wasted my time. I would give the ocean a chance. But I was in no hurry to do it. I dawdled over my breakfast, studied the paper while the meal settled, wrote a few letters home. The morning was half gone before I went out to see what this ocean had to offer.

'Now the ocean was bright – intolerably bright. Every wave was picked out by the sun. It was hard for me to look over that way. In any case, my attention was absorbed by the toilsome business of walking in the sand, for I was too ignorant to go down to where the sand had been flattened by the tides. I trudged along the beach for about a mile, scarcely conscious of the enormous presence of the sea and the multitudinous uproar of the surf, but with my head bowed to direct my steps through the difficult sand.

'Finally I judged that I had gone far enough. The hotel was out of sight beyond the curve of the shore. There was no human trace around me. I had the ocean to myself. I sat down with my back against a wind-scalloped hollow in a bank of sand, and with my face to the water.

'The prospect before me was all in motion. The waves slapped the beach, the clouds moved right to left across the sky, and the sun was hoisted, by insensible jerks, toward the zenith. All this mechanical busyness! It served to estrange me. The seascape was to me as I would be to a swarm of protozoans in the field of a microscope – that is, we had nothing to do with one another. The microcosm cannot have commerce with the macrocosm. The ocean was potent, huge and grand, but what was that to me?

'Yet even as I framed these thoughts the ocean was at work on me. The sun was warm on my face, and as I watched the endless reciprocation of the waves I became drowsy, listlessly aware of the weight of my body, a weight that seemed to grow diffuse without growing less, as if the physical stuff of me were becoming vast and tenuous. The sky was white-blue, without depth, and the sound of the ocean seemed to arise in my own inner ear. I thought I felt the ground under me rock gently this way and that, as if I were buoyed on water. All of this was pleasant – you can have no idea how pleasant. But stealthily, as I drowsed, there arose, without me or within me, some portentous thing. My breath was drawn from me. I prepared to drown in the bosom of God.

'But in that instant there was a twist, a half-turn, within me or not within me – how can I describe it? I found myself sitting stark upright, sea and sky suddenly clamorous, the sun fiercely bright; and sea, sky and sun lay like a clockwork toy in the hollow of my hand.'

Dr. Swarthmore paused, turning his gaze from right to left over the heads of his congregation.

'Then it was gone,' he continued. 'My hands were empty. Everything was as it had been. The sea scoured the sand, the sun beat upon them both. These things occurred without reference to me. They had no effect upon me, nor I upon them.

'Indeed, my estrangement from the landscape was now so complete that I had trouble believing I was in it. I seemed to be staring at an enormous chromo. Yet a moment ago this prospect and I had struggled to contain or consume one another.

'This idea ran on in silence. I didn't know what to do with it. Finally the story of Jonah came to mind. As I dozed in the sun, I had come to feel as Jonah may have felt when he was swallowed by God's great fish: a slow and unctuous passage through Leviathan's enfolding gullet, possibly not an unpleasant trip at all. I am sure that many of you would enjoy it. But in the last moment I had felt as Jonah would have felt if on the verge – the very lip – of Leviathan's stomach, of the oblivion there, he had contrived to swallow the whale.'

Again Dr. Swarthmore paused, pursing and unpursing his lips as if he were uncertain of how to proceed.

'My friends,' he said finally, 'suppose the devil came to get you. What would you do about it? You would rush to fill the space between the devil and yourself with whatever came to hand – the door, furniture, crockery, smoke, prayer, magic, propitiation, disbelief. Or maybe you'd interpose your mother-in-law. Ha ha. Well, the thing that had happened to me was nothing less than the devil, though *how* it was the devil wasn't altogether clear to me, nor did I take time to work it out. Instead I groped wildly and came up with Jonah – Jonah did the trick. My Jonah-analogy displaced the matter from the dangerous sphere of the immediate and the actual, nudged it toward the coolness and safety of abstraction. It also served to detach the matter from myself, by transferring my role to Jonah. Finally, my analogy devalued the event: the overwhelming fact of the world in my hand became a comic picture of Jonah unlimbering his whiskery jaws to accommodate the whale.

'We see in this, my friends, the vanity of the intellect. In order to master experience, it is necessary to diminish it – indeed, for the human worm, mastery and diminution are synonymous. In this respect, Jonah served me admirably: my application of Jonah leached all of the power and portent out of the episode, and the residue was a joke.

'And so I stood up from the sand and walked back to the hotel, nothing but sunny pedestrian musings in my head, anticipating nothing more portentous than a game of billiards.

'But just as indigestion will at midnight bring to the mouth a

remote, subterranean and yet distinctly feral aftertaste of supper, so I felt, as I read in my room that night, a remote but savage twinge of rage, perfectly lucid and diminished only by
being remote, as if hundreds and hundreds of miles within me
some beast all teeth and rage had torn suddenly at my heart. I
remembered then a greater rage: the rage I had felt, but at no
moment until this moment acknowledged, when the living
world had torn itself from my hand. For an instant then I had
raged, raged. You can't conceive of it. Why, the lot of you
would curl up like sow-bugs at the first whiff of it!

'But what had stirred that rage? What had I lost? I closed
my book and laid it carefully at my elbow, and my brain
swarmed like a hive. I had to think this over carefully – had to
think very carefully. It had something to do with the world,
with myself and the world. I had been shown the world – no, I
had seen the world – no, I had *held* the world. I had held the
world in my hand, and I might have crushed it as one might
crush a chick in its shell. The world had become wholly object
to my subject. The world had imploded upon me, to exist in no
other wise but in the endless concentricity of its relations to me.
What I had lost, in losing the world, was an absolute, complete
and altogether gratifying apprehension of the me-ness of *me.*'

'Thunder! I was rooted to my chair, appalled. Although this
exposition could not recover the experience it described, in contrast to even the unfleshed idea of that lost epiphany of self I
felt eerily tenuous and unreal. I floated like my own revenant in
the silence of the room. And yet I could not but feel that it was
all ridiculous – that it hadn't happened – could not have happened. It violated, intolerably, the inherent economy of things,
in which God and man keep their respective places, and neither
violates the sphere of the other. And this scrupulous reflection
restored, somewhat, the wonted placidity of my mind and tem-
per. I turned to take up my book.

'But again, and with savage impatience, the buried beast
tugged at my entrails. Fool! Fool! Fool! it cried – consider what

you've lost! And consider, I added, with tumescent fury, consider how you've lost it! My apprehension of the world in my hand had fallen away even as it had manifested itself, as if I had lacked the strength or the courage to sustain it. A self-savaging rage of disappointment, whose echo was upon me now, had assumed the place of the thing lost. But my mind, seeing its danger, had sought to diminish this cannibal disappointment by diminishing the experience whose loss had engendered it. It was fortunate, I reflected now, that it had succeeded, else I had burned my brains black with rage. But my mind had cooled me, cooled me down; betrayed the event into a conception, and cooled me.'

Dr. Swarthmore paused, unmoving, and scowled down the aisle that divided the double file of pews.

'Now, in my room,' he continued, 'now I suffered an after-taste of that rage – ashes of ashes! But I was grateful for it. For from this echo or memory of my rage, I was able to infer the magnitude of the rage itself; and the magnitude of the rage implied the magnitude of the exultation whose loss had provoked the rage. I saw now what a vast heathenish shape that exultation had been – but now my mind contained it, coldly. Contained the idea of it. Contained the ghost of that swollen, monstrous, carnivorous thing. I knew, bleakly, that I should be glad to die of this thing, if in the moment of dying I might have it back again.

'But this was unendurable. My mind recoiled from this knowledge – this revelation of the utter paganism at its core – in a kind of pietistic reflex: so this was how one lost one's soul!

'Lost one's soul indeed. But my coward mind, desperate with fear of itself, seized gratefully upon this formula, and it followed patly that I was ashamed – oh, damply, cravenly ashamed, fear and shame bursting upon me like a gout of hot blood; red, killing shame, all the power of my rage perverted to the lickspittle uses of that shame, shame for my infidel pride, fear of it, fear of its brutal avidity and its glutton pleasure in itself, the grinning, slavering toothiness and insatiability of it! This was shame indeed, you people, shame no less than the pride that had invoked it. For it took a great quantity of shame to neutralize that pride.

'Yet for all the pain of it, the purpose of this shame was not to consume me, but rather to preserve me from being consumed. It was a functional shame, a facile shame, and its substance was mechanically displaced by a sense that my sin had been remitted. Or rather I felt as if I had been passed through some sort of constrictive unctuousness, some smooth, lubricious tract from which I was voided in the end sheathed in innocence. Slathered with it. I was indeed a Jonah, but I had not left the whale by its mouth.

'While this disgusting thing was happening to me, I had no sense at all of my surroundings. I came to myself again to find myself draped bonelessly in my chair, a vapid grin on my face, perfect peace in my bosom. I jumped to my feet, shuddering as that monstrous tranquillity drained out of me. I was as hollow as a statue, weak as a child, but for the first time that day I was truly my own master. I knew now, without a doubt, that I had been *had*.

'Friends, I had been sold. The episode that had begun on the beach that morning was only now complete. My defence had been pierced, my sentinels seduced or bought – my own timid mind had several times betrayed me. A fraud had been worked upon me – or I had worked a fraud upon myself – so that in the end I would sustain a condition of being that was, to me, as novel as it was repellent: the peace of perfect union with God.

'Or, at least, a condition that some people might call by that name. I was not yet willing to concede that God had anything to do with it. The macrocosm cannot have commerce with the microcosm! And yet – I wasn't sure. I wasn't sure! For the first time in my life, I felt the gnawing of those hideous corrosives, perplexity and doubt. I paced my narrow room, door to window, window to door, but so great was my confusion that now and again I forgot what I was confused *about*. What could it be that had made me so distraught? Was I worried about money? About where I had put the return half of my train ticket? No – and then, you see, I would remember – no, I was brooding on God, man, grace, oceans, epiphanies.... Thunder! It wasn't like me at all.

'Now, with my confusion there grew a loathing of the inno-cent appurtenances of my room. The walls seemed to press upon my forehead as I approached them. The bed, the chair, the wardrobe offended me: I wanted to kick them. Finally I wrenched open the door, flung it with gratifying violence against the wall and went from the place, a goaded bull. It was fortunate, perhaps, that I met no one on the stairs or in the lobby. Nor was there anyone on the long veranda that ran behind the hotel. I had it to myself.

'The noise of the surf reached the porch, but the sea itself was invisible in the darkness – hiding itself out my sight, per-haps, for I had half a mind to go down and wrestle with it, like Achilles in his madness. Instead, I paced the porch up and down, up and down, and at last I was able to address the prob-lem that confronted me with something like my accustomed coolness and calm.

'It came down to this: either the thing had been done to me or I had done it to myself. The first alternative was horrible. I had never solicited the gift of grace, and yet it had come to me. Presumably it could come to me again, and there was nothing I could do about it. At any moment God might obliterate me in his embrace.

'On the other hand, if the second alternative described the case – if I had done this dreadful thing to myself – then I was a suggestible fool, given to transcendental fits.

'For some time I pondered these alternatives. I was either a fool of God or my own fool. On the whole, I liked it better the second way, but I didn't like it much.

'I stopped pacing. I had remembered – how had I forgotten?

– the other aspect of the day's experience. I had suffered an intrusion of grace on the beach this morning, and I had suffered a second and more conclusive intrusion in my room just now. But I had also, for an instant, enjoyed a taste of quite some other thing, whatever the word for it might be. And that taste had been like meat to a cannibal. I wanted more of it. If I were obliged to believe that God had subverted me, I would do it with a will, for then it must also be true (and I remembered, with cold exultance, the world in my hand) that I had subverted God.

'This enormous conclusion advanced itself boldly. There it was. My mind, seeing the fatal audacity of the thing, hesitated to take it – hesitated, I say, but did not spurn it or shrink from it. Nevertheless I hesitated, and as I hesitated I found myself listening to the surf. Such a monotonous, mechanical sound! It conveyed to me the idea of measureless volumes of inanimate ocean, whose cold slackness consumed, over and over and over again, all of the creatures that it sustained, even as. the dead earth sustains and consumes us. The sea was a blankness: no agency, not even the intelligence that had made it, could use it as an instrument of its will.

'Therefore (I decided, taking up my march along the porch again) – therefore, what had happened to me on the beach was an accident, and what had happened since I had perpetrated on myself. The sun and the sea had acted on me, but they had acted obliviously; no *conscious* external force had worked to undo me. Nothing had followed from my dozing in the sand that could not be dismissed as a product of my own mind – as my mind's disordered response to an aspect of creation that was new to it. Simply my prejudices, my susceptibilities – those tumbled flints – striking sparks from one another.

'But this was preposterous. I might be a fool, but I was not fool enough to have let myself play such a trick on myself. Of course, only my agreement that I was just as much of a fool as I could be would allow me to preserve my old belief in

45

the neutrality of Providence and hence justify my own cherished neutrality of spirit. But the fact was that I no longer wished to be neutral. If I denied my near-obliteration in God, I had also to deny the world's near-obliteration in *me*. But if the one thing had happened, then the other thing had happened too.

'So the day's experience had converted me. I flung my neutrality aside like a dirtied clout. I claimed my spiritual dividend. What had happened to me that morning was a revelation – not an accident, not a delusion, but a revelation, a disclosure, a rending of the veil. You people may think it strange that I should have made so much of a moment's confusion on a beach. But I say to you that all things are portentous, all things signify. Therefore never hesitate to snatch up your sheet of tin and roll out some thunder on it!

'Very well. I had no doubts now about *what* had happened. It remained to determine *how* it had happened. For unless I understood the *how* of the matter I would be able neither to resist further onslaughts of Providence nor to make any onslaughts of my own. My task, therefore, was to apply myself closely to the dynamics of the experience, to puzzle out the machinery of it. Most of the experience, as I understood it now, had been not my doing but God's doing, and my own momentary contribution had been responsive rather than initiatory. I would begin, accordingly, not with the interior mechanism but with the exterior one – the mechanism of divine aggression.

'Two assaults had been made on me. The first I had somehow repelled. I had invited it, apparently, by sitting passively in the sand, with no particular thought or feeling in me. The second intrusion, by contrast, had followed upon a condition of feeling more vehement, perhaps, than any I had previously sustained – an exaggerated sense of shame.

'Now, what did this spasm of shame and the business of dozing in the sun have in common? Why, in both situations I had entertained a vastly diminished sense of myself; that is, my *self*.

In the first instance, I had allowed that self to be eroded away by the elements of sensible nature. I had drowsed under the sun, and the sun had worked upon me; under the sun's warmth I had relaxed, as it were, into the liquid essence of myself, and I was, accordingly, and by small degrees, absorbed into the sand, sucked into vapour by the air. Thus, gently, God had sipped me, drunk me into his substance –'

As Dr. Swarthmore described this process, his gaze lost its focus, his voice its resonance. Finally he was silent, rocking gently on his heels. A man in one of the rear pews stood up.

'Dr. Swarthmore,' he said, 'It strikes me that there's something devilishly heterodox about the drift of this so-called sermon of yours, especially this latest business. Are you sure you're not a pantheist?'

'My friend,' Dr. Swarthmore replied, leaning over the pulpit, 'I see that you are a stranger. It's plain, moreover, that you hail from some place far larger and grander than our little town.

'Well, when you get back to Springfield or Cincinnati or Chicago, or wherever it is you come from, I hope you'll remember without *too* much condescension the sample of good old country sermonizing that I've dished out to these folks today. But to deal with the point you raise, the fact is that you've misconstrued – wilfully too, it seems to me – what I've been saying here. No, friend, I do not – and did not, even at the time about which I've been speaking – I did not make the direful mistake of confusing the creator with his creation. But insofar as that creation is God's agency or vehicle – the projection of his being, I could say, much as our habitual grimaces, our turns of speech, our tastes in clothing, houses, shoes, furniture, haircuts and wallpaper give each of us an externalized being, a small creation essentially his own, by means of which he manifests himself to his fellows and is known to them – as I say, insofar as God's creation is the reflection or shadow of God, I think it is permitted to me to say that as I sat on the beach God worked upon me and I was nearly lost in God. That will do, I think. You don't agree? Well, take it easy, fellow. I may have touched dubious ground once or twice in the course of this thing, but it all winds up in a perfect fit of orthodoxy – you'll see.

'But to return to my thoughts as I walked the porch. I had observed, you'll remember, that my unmindfulness of myself as I drowsed in the sand had made me prey for God. In the second instance, in my room that night, I had deliberately scoured myself of myself, using shame for an abrasive. In both instances I had left myself exposed to any agency that was itself free to invade me. 'But why had the second assault succeeded where the first had failed? And why had the first intrusion failed in such an extraordinary way? Why hadn't I simply shaken it off? I had on other occasions, in musing upon outward nature, drifted into just such a state of imbecile reverie, in which it was not clear to me where my surroundings left off and I began. But on these occasions I had simply let the thing run on for a time and then bestirred myself and gone about my business. On *this* occasion, I had passed far beyond the state in which my will could operate casually – or, indeed, operate at all. It was as if the intruding force had worn away all of the concentric layers of my soul, had dissolved my very will itself, had only to lap once at the small grain of my being's core in order to nullify me altogether – but in touching that grain had instead provoked some mysterious energy latent in it. In that instant, the force directed against me had become mine to direct against the aggressor. And even as it had become mine it had acted, and put the world into my hand. And even as it acted it was expended. The world and I were discrete entities again, neither possessing the other, and I sprawled witless and raging in the sand.

'Now, as I walked the porch, I was struck by the impossibility of this dynamic. One might more plausibly suppose that a hurtling locomotive could of an instant reverse its direction without abating its speed. How could *I* have reversed a process that had the whole authority of Providence behind it? The force of this objection was such that I was again obliged to doubt whether Providence had had anything to do with it. No doubt the whole affair was, after all, an absurdity that I had perpetrated on myself.

'I don't recall how long I turned the matter over, shifting the alternatives from hand to hand. But finally my thoughts led me to a remote ancestor of mine, my six-times-great-grandfather, a clergyman who had been driven out of England by the Romanizing innovations of Archbishop Laud. This ancestor had comforted his exile by publishing, through an English printer in Amsterdam, several bulky volumes of sermons. It may seem strange to you – what does not? – that people ever troubled to put sermons into anything more enduring than the weekly newspaper. My ancestor, however, lived in urgent and portentous times. To the divines of that age, it seemed that the urgency would end only with the world itself; that later generations – if there were to be later generations – would continue to feel God's own hot breath in every word that had ever been uttered over the top of a pulpit. So their words were put into books, books filled with quarrelsome and intemperate voices. Our religion was a bursting star, then, and each mote within that anarchy of light flew alone toward the boundaries of the created sphere. Certain forces strained to hold the centre, but still the thing swelled and flew apart, throwing off a fiery heat and a light that was no more brilliant collectively than it was in detail; for each mote, each man was filled with light, filled as full as he could be, and therefore filled with all of the light there is – a passion of conviction that astonishes us into incredulity, now. We are more careful. We know better than to be sure. But our ancestors lived in a warmer age, and had hot hearts. They would, perhaps, find us to be a tepid, cautious and mean-spirited lot, our faith pallid and chilly. But every age has its peculiar temperature, and need not apologize to any other age.

'All the same, my ancestor was none of your boneless, mild, dishwater Christians of the modern sort, but a Christian made

49

like a Visigoth. His portrait, which hangs in my study, shows a long carnivorous jaw, a broad trap of mouth and strong yellow teeth made for grinding sectaries of a tenderer composition. The eyes are sunken and colourless. The eyebrows and hair are a bold, barbarian red, and between them the forehead is both broad and high, and as white as bone.

'Altogether, this ancestor looks both uncouth and proud; looks more than commonly susceptible to all of the grosser sins, and to arrogance of mind as well. Yet if we are to believe the record he has left – those sermons and whatnot – he was scarcely a being of flesh and bone, but rather one three parts gone to incandescence. The brain within his heavy skull – a subtle and passionate brain, to be sure – was wrapped concupiscently around the kernel of God.

'There is no exaggerating the intensity and the exclusiveness of his obsessive faith. Wife, children and fortune were all subordinate to a vision of the white-limbed soul's yielding to the ardent Lord, the athletic and everlasting Christ. The language in which he clothed his faith sounds a little peculiar now – a little unseemly, in fact, and for that reason I apologize in advance for what I shall now read to you:

' "O, my terrible Lord, I behold Thy coming! I hear Thy tread ring upon the stones of the floor, and in my small, poor chamber I tremble, weeping and afraid; my breast flutters, my mouth is dry, my knees will not uphold me. But when I see Thy luminous countenance, the smooth comeliness of Thy limbs – O, Thou strikest my breath from me! I gasp, and fill my throat with Thy milky sweetness –"

'And so forth. A bold apostrophe, but my ancestor did not invent it. Any number of radical divines used the device, in one paraphrase or another, to dramatize the soul's commerce with God. Still, it is peculiar that so active, vigorous and, by all accounts, coarse and even violent a man as my ancestor was should have chosen to advertise his soul as a shrinking, passive and girlish thing. As a young man, I was profoundly dismayed by this contradiction. I could find no way in which to reconcile my ancestor's distressing rhetoric with the face in the portrait, which seemed to have edged a little closer to the brutes every time I looked at it. It wasn't until I walked the porch that night, alternately marvelling at my own soul's victory over an aggressive Providence and wondering if Providence had been in it at all, that I guessed his motive for using language of this kind to express his intercourse with God.

'In the sexual act, with which some of you are doubtless familiar, isn't it moot, finally, who prevails over whom? Here's your ardent swain, moved by a sweet aggressiveness to seize and enter the yielding – or, for that matter, the resisting – body of his mistress. It is he who initiates the act, he who invades and despoils, and so it would seem that it's all pretty much his show. But let us consider the end of the business: our swain lies spent and confused; his consort, meanwhile, has absorbed his boldest thunder and secreted it in her belly, perhaps to nurture it there – not unmoved, not unshaken by that thunder, yet on the whole composed. Now what has happened between the first and the last but a displacement of control, the drowning or envelopment of the lover's assault in the vessel of his mistress's flesh?

'It was a dangerous notion, but one that I could not forbear from voicing to myself as I stalked the porch, walked it up and down, that in the same way, perhaps, God hurls himself upon our souls and is lost. And we assume his power. He becomes an imp bottled in our skulls, wholly ours to possess and control. It was this that my ancestor knew, and it was this that I had accomplished, all unknowing and for a moment only, upon the beach that morning.

'Now, what an idea, what a conceit! This ancestor had been a lunatic – that was plain – and yet I was tempted to share his lunacy. Perhaps I was obliged to share it, for it seemed that it could not believe in the active agency of God unless I also believed in my own power to contend against his agency. It seemed, indeed, that to declare one's faith in a living God was to declare war on him: one allowed one's soul to become the bride of Christ, but only in order to treat him as Jael had treated Sisera. One's victory could not be final, perhaps, but there could be moments – moments of the kind I had enjoyed on the beach; and these moments could, perhaps, be extended or, at least, invoked with some frequency.

'Again, what a conceit. Gingerly, I savoured it. I walked the porch, I, the subduer of God, and felt the idea glow in my belly. Only by degrees was that warmth displaced by an insinuating chill, a slowly uncoiling dread that suggested, remotely and coolly, that I bear in mind the outcome of my day's adventures. Didn't I recall the condition in which I had found myself only a little while ago, up in my room? I slowed my walk, midway on the porch. Why yes, I recalled it perfectly. Well then – my entrails spoke again – how did I account for it? Wasn't it possible that the taste of God I had enjoyed in the morning had been bait, bait for a trap that had taken the whole long day to close upon me?

'I spoke boldly against this inward voice. Of course there had been a trap. But the question was, could God have captured me had my own mind not connived with him in the working of his trap? God had been unable to carry the assault against me even when I lay passive and drowsy in the sun; indeed, it had appeared for a moment that the contest would go quite the other way. That God had accomplished his object later was a tribute less to his power than to his guile; it showed that he had, in the interval, found an instrument that enabled him to do his work – and what could that instrument have been, save my own treacherous mind? I reached the end of the porch, turned, and started back again. Of course. I had suspected this before – I saw it clearly now. God had found an ally in my mind's own fear of itself, its fear of the blasphemous powers that had been revealed to it on the beach; powers against which God himself could not prevail. My timid, treacherous mind, or rather the part of it that had been debilitated

by a long pickling in the fear of God and in the habits of a religion that was the codification of this fear – this poor, craven
morsel of my being had, in the coward hope of obtaining some
crumb of favour from the God it feared, subverted me, conspired
with God to translate me into oblivion, to sell me out of myself.
Why, with his odious object achieved, God had chosen to withdraw, to leave me to myself again, I did not know – perhaps so
that I might reflect upon how easily he had achieved my ruin,
how readily he might achieve it again, given half my being as an
ally.

' "All right, then," I said aloud, vehemently treading the
porch. "I give you today's contest. *You* have won – today. But
henceforth I shall deny you your ally. I shall purge myself of the
traitor in me. I shall dismember my soul to thwart you. I shall
throttle any slightest murmur of propitiation that might try to
escape me. Not the smallest grain of worship will you extort from
me. I know my powers now. Why should I purchase my destruction to obtain your favour? We shall see who consumes whom."

'The interior voice spoke for the last time: Have it your own
way, it said, but by whose favour, then, will you take one more
step on this porch?

'I stopped walking, cataleptic with dread. A horrible void –
not a hole, less than a hole – had opened where I was about to
step. Then was revealed to me the brute mechanical power of
God, his boundless and ineluctable dominion over me, over the
very roots of my hair, over every atom and particle of me. A
knowledge so final, so terrific, that I fell swooning to the floor.
Which was, by the grace of God, there to receive me.

'So I exhort you: praise God and fear him. I am done.'

On his way out of the church, Blount paused at a little table
that stood just inside the door. A variety of devotional litera-
ture, including Dr. Swarthmore's pamphlet, was displayed
upon the table, next to a cigar box with a slot cut in the lid. It
was Blount's habit to buy a copy of any new publication that
the table had to offer.

The crack under Blount's door showed light into the small hours. No sound came from the room. The landlady, wondering if he had died, put her eye to the keyhole.

So preternaturally motionless, so silent and rigid was Blount, seated at his round oak table, that it took the landlady a moment to realize that the room was occupied. Above the table hung a lamp, a big, nickel-plated pressure lamp that burned with a remote submarine roar. Its solar glare, circumscribed by a conical tin shade, discovered the minutest detail of every object, including the front portion of Blount, that stood within a foot or two of the table; the rest of the room, however, abode in Egyptian darkness. A sense of the room's dimensions was something that the landlady had to supply from her previous experience of the place: there was nothing she could point to, now, to prove that the darkness beyond the field of the lamp was not coextensive with the night's own vast indeterminacy. Blount sat three paces from the door, as upright as a flagpole, with his hands invisible in the abrupt darkness under the table. His profile was turned toward the keyhole, and the line of the light fell just forward of his ear; hence the top and the back of his head were invisible as well. He stared at a little book, or booklet, that lay open on the glossy table top. The lamp – aloof divinity of this pocket universe – roared like the sea in a seashell.

Blount's hand shot out of the darkness and turned the page. Then the hand was gone and he was motionless again. This motionlessness was so complete that the contemplation of it stealthily detached the landlady from her volition. She settled her weight on her calves, swayed a little and became as motionless as Blount was.

* * *

If time is the product of change, then the subtlest observer in the world would have been hard put to find evidence that time was passing in the context whose elements were Blount, his lamp, his table, his book and the taxidermical landlady propped against the keyhole. The only events were Blount's turnings of pages, and the movements that created these events were so rapid and mechanical, like the tongue-dartings of a frog, that the observer would have been no more certain than the landlady was that he had seen them.

Slight as the events were, though, they were sufficient. The left-hand accumulation of pages grew thicker and the right-hand accumulation correspondingly attenuate. The effect was to inform the context with a kind of objective suspense – a quality of inexorable tendency that existed without reference to Blount or his landlady or even to the hypothetical observer of the whole. But it was a tendency that was in no hurry to disclose its object. Blount and his book floated unceasingly within the parabolic fall of lamplight, and the light itself floated like an egg in the unbounded darkness of the room.

* * *

The last page had been turned. The book lay closed. The landlady felt shooting pains in her thighs. She generated rancour through the keyhole. But surely he would do something now.

Blount was cast in lead. His gaze did not shift by the width of a hair. Then, with no augmentation of its roar, the lamp above the table flared. A gorgeous fragmentation of light, a glamour of hard static light escaped the boundary of the lamp's field to stand irradiant from the dark crown of Blount's head. The landlady tottered backwards and fell. Her hands scrabbled silently on the carpeted floor. She rolled over and raised herself onto her knees and hands. She gaped wildly at the door. Then, still on her knees, she scuttled away to the head of the stairs and was gone.

The Notebook

On Monday evening Dr. Swarthmore's housekeeper admitted Blount to her employer's study. Here were three walls covered with bookcases, a coal fire in a microscopic fireplace and Dr. Swarthmore himself, ambushed behind a large desk of fumed oak. The room was small and almost unendurably well-lit: an electric chandelier fitted with seven flame-shaped bulbs had hunted down and extirpated every scrap of shadow in the place. An observer would have noted that under this glare both Blount and Dr. Swarthmore looked curiously flat and flimsy, like a couple of playing cards. But there was no observer: the Doctor's housekeeper, unlike Blount's landlady, knew how to mind her own business.

Dr. Swarthmore went on reading for half a minute or so after Blount had entered the room. Then he turned down a corner of the page and pushed the book aside.

'I found a note of yours with the afternoon mail.' The Doctor's voice was at once crisp and resonant, with a quality at the bottom of it like a shout heard from far away. 'You say you want to discuss something.' He showed his teeth. 'Something *important*, hay?'

Blount advanced a step.

'Yes, Dr. Swarthmore.' He was all dimples – yet grave. 'It's a matter of mutual advantage – yours and mine, I mean.'

'Mutual advantage, hay?'

'It's that pamphlet of yours, Doctor.'

'My pamphlet, hay? What about it?'

'There's money in it.'

Dr. Swarthmore sucked on his rubbery underlip.

'Say that again, Blount.'

'I said there's money in it.'

'Money!' A long pause followed this word. 'In what sense is there money in it?'

'In the sense that people will buy it, sir.'

'People will buy it.' Another pause. 'Why would they do that?'

Blount cleared his throat. 'Well, Dr. Swarthmore, as you may or may not know, I do a lot of selling around here – books, notions, sewing machines, anything folks will buy. I'm pretty good at it. It's a natural talent, you could say.' He looked modestly at the floor.

'Then you're a lucky young fellow, Blount.' The Doctor spoke with just a touch of irony. 'But what exactly do you mean? Do you mean that you're good at talking people into buying things they don't want? Or do you mean you're good at guessing what they do want, and hence you have it on hand for them to buy? You see the difference, hay?'

Blount looked a little hurt. 'More the second thing, Dr. Swarthmore, though it takes a bit of work sometimes to make it clear to people what it is they want.'

'Ha, ha,' said the Doctor, and he showed his teeth again. 'That was dry, Blount, very dry. But let me see if I have it right. When you say that people will buy my pamphlet you don't mean that you – you for example, that is – that you'd have to stuff it down their throats. You mean rather that the pamphlet does address a need, or at any rate a wish. That a demand for a commodity of this sort exists. Is this what you're suggesting?'

'More or less, Dr. Swarthmore. You see, I keep my eyes open. I've noticed things.' The things that Blount had noticed were, first, a sensible increase in attendance at both the college chapel and Dr. Swarthmore's church in town and, at the same time, a sensible decrease in contributions to the building and missionary funds; second, a sharp decline in the number of collegians who departed on the Friday afternoon train for weekends of metropolitan hijinks in Indianapolis; and, third, a growing reluctance among his customers to buy goods, such as justified only by extended use. On the other hand, he was doing a land-rush business in Bibles and firearms. What Blount had detected, in short, was the percolation through the neighbourhood of a generalized unease. Something was on people's minds.

'I see what you're driving at, I think,' said Dr. Swarthmore, pursing his lips in a speculative way. 'But isn't it possible that you're seeing connections where none exist? Consider these matters separately, and each of them might be separately explained. Explained, moreover, in a perfectly commonplace way.' The Doctor suggested that worry about the weather or the hog cholera or the Chicago market or any of the hundred things that farmers were always worrying about was responsible for their reluctance to invest in parlour organs for their wives. Maybe, said Blount, but the fact was that the corn was in, the hogs were in good health and pork was thirteen cents a pound. Dr. Swarthmore observed that the approach of mid-term examinations might reasonably be expected to keep the student body away from the fleshpots for the time being. Blount begged his pardon, but he was obliged to point out that as a rule it worked quite the other way. Finally the doctor himself conceded that the rise in church attendance (he was taking Blount's word for it) was a circumstance wholly out of the ordinary.

So Dr. Swarthmore agreed that the changes to which Blount had referred might indeed arise from a single cause. It was difficult, however, to say what that cause might be. There had been no epidemics, floods or tornadoes of late, no gangs of tramps or arsonists abroad, no Anarchists agitating among the harvest hands. In short, nothing to threaten either the prosperity or the tranquillity of the neighbourhood. So if people *did* have something on their minds, some apprehension compelling enough to modify their behaviour, this apprehension was, as yet, provisional. It still awaited its object. People were expecting something to happen, but they had no explicit notion of what that something was.

'That's it exactly,' Blount put in, and he went on to make his pitch. Its essence was this:

Since nothing else answered, the public's anxiety could only be a response to the approach of the century's end – to the imminence of that end, the ineluctable certainty of it. The times were portentous by definition. Of course, no one knew what it was that he expected. Indeed, no one knew that he expected anything. Yet however thin and unspecific this climate of expectation might be, it was exploitable. There was money in it. He, Blount, had drawn this conclusion some time ago. All that was needed was a vessel into which the expectation could pour itself and assume an explicit shape. The money would come from providing that vessel. Dr. Swarthmore's pamphlet had fallen into his hands, and he had seen at once that it would do the trick. The pamphlet was a lens through which expectation could be projected and resolved. A tangible dread was a less uncomfortable possession than a shapeless anxiety, so the pamphlet would serve, in effect, as a means of relief, like a purgative or a headache powder. Therefore people would buy it. The pamphlet wasn't an ideal commodity. There was too much of the peculiar in it, especially toward the end. But it was adequate. It would do. In any case, a well-conducted sales campaign would compensate for its deficiencies.

Dr. Swarthmore followed this exposition with the air of a man whose hard-headed skepticism yielded only to the soundest arguments – but who was forced, in this instance, to admit that every argument rang with the obstinate credibility of a silver dollar. When Blount was finished, the Doctor indicated by various tokens – nods, grunts, thoughtful tuggings at the corner of his beard – that if he wasn't convinced yet, he was willing to be. Blount, never one to let an advantage grow stale, got right down to the facts and figures.

'Dr. Swarthmore,' said Blount, looking hard at that party, 'what do you suppose the population of this county is?' Under the cover of this question, he moved a step closer to the desk.

'Why, I don't know, Blount,' Dr. Swarthmore replied. 'I never thought about it.'

'Doctor, according to the United States Bureau of the Census, the population of this county in 1890 was' – his hand went briskly to the inside pocket of his coat and brought out a small notebook, which he flicked open with his thumb – 'seventeen thousand six hundred and thirty-seven persons.' So orotund was Blount's recitation of this figure that it seemed almost to count off each of those seventeen thousand and more, and to list their names and birthdays too.

'As many as that,' said Dr. Swarthmore, and his eyes grew a trifle more wide. 'Well, well.'

'There's been a bit of growth in the past ten years. Suppose we round that figure to twenty thousand.'

'Very well, we'll round it,' the Doctor said.

'Twenty thousand people. Say five to the household. I make that four thousand households in the county, Dr. Swarthmore.'

'Your arithmetic's unimpeachable, Blount.'

'Four thousand households,' Blount said again, drawing the juice out of it. 'Now, suppose I were to place a copy of your pamphlet in every one of those four thousand households. How would you feel about that?'

Dr. Swarthmore pursed and unpursed his lips a couple of times. 'Well, Blount, I guess I would be obliged to feel gratified.'

Blount, who had been closing in on Dr. Swarthmore's desk all through this exchange, now retreated to his starting point.

'Dr. Swarthmore,' he began again, when he was back in his place, 'how many people do you figure there are in the State of Indiana?'

'I don't know, Blount. Do you?'

Blount opened his notebook again. 'The census for 1890 gives the figure two million three hundred and forty-five thousand nine hundred and fifty-two.'

'That many! No, Blount, I won't believe it – you're voting the graveyards.'

Blount looked hurt. 'Doctor, these are official government figures.'

'You're right – how stupid of me. I apologize, Blount. Proceed.'

'Two million three hundred and forty-five thousand nine hundred and fifty-two.' The number rolled out like distant summer thunder. 'That was ten years ago. Suppose we round it to two and a half million.'

'Round away, Blount.'

'Five people to the household ...'

'That's reasonable, Blount – perfectly reasonable.'

'... makes a round five hundred thousand households.'

'Round! Orbicular, Blount, absolutely orbicular!'

'Dr. Swarthmore –' once again Blount was right up to the desk '– I told you before that I could bury this county in pamphlets – four thousand pamphlets.'

'A large figure, Blount – gratifyingly large.'

'Well, forget it, Doctor, it's nothing.' Blount dismissed the four thousand with a wave of his hand.

Dr. Swarthmore was silent for a moment, with his lips pursed. 'You're right, Blount,' he said finally. 'Four thousand – it *seemed* like a large number when you first brought it up, but I see now what a nugatory trifle it is. As you say – nothing.'

'Instead, Dr. Swarthmore, I want you to think about *one half million* pamphlets – one in every house and dwelling in Indiana.'

'Blount, you take my breath away.'

'And that's not counting the slopover into Illinois and Ohio – there's a market there too, I'll bet.'

'You're piling wonders on wonders, Blount.'

'Furthermore, Doctor, there'll be no need to approach any publisher or distributor or whatever to get the job done. I'll handle every detail myself.'

'You!'

'Well, sure. Me.' And Blount looked so meek and guileless that he was nearly invisible.

'That's all very self-confident of you, Blount, but where are your means for carrying out such an enterprise? You have no outlets, no agents, no transport –'

'No, you're wrong there, Dr. Swarthmore, if you don't mind my saying so. I have – or I can get – all of those things, or what I need of them. It's all right at hand.'

'Blount, this is obfuscation. Speak plainly.'

'Fair enough, Dr. Swarthmore. I want you to work up this picture in your mind's eye: three hundred salesmen – eager beavers, every one of them – distributed over every part of the state, their movements directed from a central point by telegraph and telephone, each one of those three hundred knocking on a hundred doors every day – thirty thousand doors in a day. In a month they've darkened every door in the state. The best part of it is, most of them will do it for nothing.'

Dr. Swarthmore started out of his chair. 'Blount, you're mad. An army of drummers – working for free! I never heard such a fantasy. Where will you get this mob of philanthropic drudges – grow 'em from dragon's teeth?'

'No, Doctor.' Blount leaned his knuckles on the desk. 'The college.'

'The college! Thunder!'

'The current enrolment here is three hundred and forty-three. We'll send the whole crowd out.'

'The whole crowd!'

'Some of them will have to be paid or put on commission. Just a few. A lot won't even realize they're working. You'll see what I mean when the time comes. The rest will do it for a lark – and a pass for the term. There'll be expenses, of course, train fares and the like.'

Dr. Swarthmore held up his hand. 'Blount, stop right there. This is an abominable hoax – I smell it now. Even granting that your scheme could be realized, why would I ever agree to it? Suppose you did empty the place for a month; how would I explain the circumstance? Why, there's the faculty, the parents, the trustees. The trustees, Blount, who hold me in the hollow of their hand! Quite apart from the gross dereliction of duty in which you propose to implicate me, what makes you think I would consent to the annihilation of my livelihood?'

Instead of addressing this question, Blount consulted his notebook for a minute or so. Then he closed it and slid it into his pocket.

'Dr. Swarthmore,' he said finally, 'you're charging a dime for your pamphlet – requesting a ten-cent contribution for it, I should say. If you don't mind my asking, how much does it cost you to produce each pamphlet?'

'I don't mind at all, Blount.' The Doctor lowered himself into his chair again. 'I've had the pamphlet run off on the college's press. All I paid for was the paper and the ink. It cost me thirty dollars to run off a thousand copies. Not that I ever expect to get rid of that many.'

'Three cents a copy.'

'Correct.'

'That's a pretty good set-up, the print shop.'

'Not bad at all, Blount. Capable of far fancier work than they've done on my pamphlet, in fact.'

'They print *The American Missionary* there.'

'Well, yes, as you know perfectly well, Blount, they do indeed print *The American Missionary* there. We do that work for the Protestant Missionary Alliance – a welcome source of revenue for the college.'

'Fine magazine, *The American Missionary.*'

'The most intelligent publication of its kind in the country, Blount.'

'Good-looking, I mean. Well-produced.'

'That too, Blount. Our printing establishment is wholly up-to-date.'

'You're right about that, doctor. As a matter of fact, I stopped by there before I came over here.'

'You did, hay?'

'Yes, Dr. Swarthmore. I asked the fellow in charge there what it would cost to produce a little booklet with about as much matter in it as your pamphlet, but done up in grander style – better paper, a picture on the cover, maybe one or more inside as well. The man looked up some prices, did a little arithmetic, asked how big a run I had in mind – you know the kind of questions they ask – and in the end reckoned they could produce ten thousand copies at nine cents the copy. The price goes down little by little the farther you go beyond that initial ten thousand – it has to do with the size of the order for your paper and the like, you see. If you order a hundred thousand copies or more, you're back down to the three cents per copy you paid for those thousand copies, but you're getting a much finer product for your money. One you could charge a quarter for without being unreasonable. Now, the fellow at the shop figures that if he put his other work aside and used both rotary presses he could churn out that hundred thousand in a week. In a month he could do half a million. It would be a close thing, but he could do it. Half a million pamphlets, sold at a quarter each, would bring in $125,000. But we'll be cautious. Let's say 400,000 printed and sold, or $100,000. Printing costs would be about $12,000. Promotion, commissions and so forth shouldn't amount to more than about another $12,000. So our costs would be about $25,000, but there'll be no need to scratch the money up all at once. I figure five or six thousand will get the ball rolling, and we'll plow back the receipts to make up the rest. Anyway, deduct our costs, and we're left with a net return of $75,000.'

'Thunder!' said Dr. Swarthmore. 'You certainly do have a genius for numbers, Blount.'

Blount fished out his notebook again. 'Your present salary, Dr. Swarthmore – I got this from the trustees' last annual report – your salary is –'

'Never mind my salary, Blount. You've made your point.' The Doctor's gaze dropped to the blank surface of his desk. 'It's preposterous. I know it is. And yet there's credibility in it, somehow – even apart from my credulous willingness to believe in it. It could happen, by God!'

'It *will* happen, Dr. Swarthmore. I know it will.'

The Doctor looked up sharply. 'Ah. You know, do you? And how is it that you know?'

'It's as I said before, Doctor. I have a talent. As soon as I read your pamphlet I saw a chance to justify that talent. No, more than that. I knew that I was *obliged* to use this chance – there's necessity in it. My talent – the one I was telling you about, Dr. Swarthmore – why, that's a gift from God. Now, why was I given such a powerful gift? When I read your pamphlet I saw the answer. I'm to use my talent by collaborating with you in disclosing to the world God's plan for it. That's how it is.'

'Is it?' The Doctor showed his teeth. 'I give you credit – you got all of that out with a straight face. But tell me, is this justification or fulfilment of your so-called talent the only compensation you expect for your labour?'

Blount coloured delicately. 'Why, no, Dr. Swarthmore. I was thinking along the lines of some proportion or other of the net receipts – fifty percent, say.'

'Ah.'

'Of course, that's assuming you'll take on the initial costs. Or I can assume some part of the costs, if you like – that is, in a way. That is, I can lend you what's needed at a very reasonable rate.' The Doctor made no reply, so after a moment Blount continued. 'Not that I'm interested in the money for its own sake, Dr. Swarthmore. I'd hate to have you think that. It's just that I have to have a tangible compensation in keeping with my effort – something to measure that effort, to show that my expenditure of effort has been appropriate to my talent. As I've said, that talent is a gift from God, and I'm obliged to exploit it to the limit. And that's just what I'll do, Dr. Swarthmore, to get your pamphlet out. It's a solemn task, and not an easy one either, but I won't shrink from it. You can rest assured –'

'Oh, put it away, Blount.' The Doctor scowled. 'Give yourself a rest.' He turned slightly in his chair and opened one of the drawers of the desk.

'I'm sorry, Doctor.' Blount appeared to be slightly at a loss. 'Did you say –'

'I said you can stop talking now.' The Doctor took a tablet of ruled paper from the drawer and placed it squarely on the desk. He leaned forward, rising an inch or two out of his chair, and pulled the inkstand closer to himself. He rummaged in the drawer again, came up with a pen, scrutinized its nib against the overweening light of the chandelier, dipped it in ink.

For a time, the only sound in the room was that most businesslike of all sounds, the scratching of a steel pen. 'The fact is, Blount,' the Doctor said presently, not looking up from his sedulous pen, 'the fact is that I had a pretty good idea of what you were up to as soon as I saw your note. "What's this?" I asked myself. "The boy entrepreneur wants an interview. Could it be that he hopes to sell me a sewing machine?"' The Doctor tore the sheet from the tablet, waved it in the air, then laid it down at his elbow. He glanced at it from time to time as he applied his pen to the tablet again. 'Then I remembered seeing you pick up a copy of my pamphlet after the morning service yesterday, and lo, it all fell into place. But I want to thank you. Your coming to see me has saved me the trouble of summoning you, as I had pretty well made up my mind to do.' The Doctor stopped writing, looked from one sheet to the other several times, then tore the second sheet from the tablet and pushed it across the desk.

'We'll need my housekeeper to witness this.' The Doctor's right hand dropped out of sight, and an electric buzzer sounded somewhere in the house. 'Well, promote the pamphlet, Blount – none of your door-to-door stuff, but get it out in the open somehow – as I say, promote it effectively and you'll get fifteen percent of the profits. And no, I don't need a loan from you, thank you. I have little enough, God knows, but I can, I think, capitalize this venture out of my own resources.' Blount had picked up the second sheet of paper, looked at it and put it back on the desk.

'You're right about one thing,' Dr. Swarthmore continued, frowning thoughtfully past Blount. 'There are perhaps larger possibilities here than I had imagined. And I agree that a new edition of the pamphlet is in order. It looks so shabby as it stands that you couldn't pay people to take it. But as for papering the state – emptying the college – printing pamphlets by the bale!' The Doctor looked sternly at his partner-elect. 'Frankly, Blount, I'm surprised. I would have thought, from what I've heard about you, that you were the last person to let his enthusiasm outrun his prudence. Come in, Mrs. Finn.' The housekeeper came into the room and stood just inside the door. 'Mr. Blount and I are going to sign some papers, and we'll need you to sign them too – as a witness, you see, so that everything will be in order. Are you quite satisfied, Blount?' The Doctor put his hand into the drawer again and drew out a big, potent-looking cigar, which he rolled between his palms. Blount was motionless.

'Thirty,' he said finally.

'Twenty,' said Dr. Swarthmore.

'Twenty-five.'

'All right,' said the Doctor. He put the cigar down and scribbled briefly on each of the two sheets. 'Twenty-five per cent of the net.' He pushed both sheets across to Blount, who leaned over the desk to sign.

'Mrs. Finn? If you please? We'll start working out the details tomorrow, Blount. Thank you, Mrs. Finn. You may go. We have, let's see, less than five months until the equinox, five months in which to make our fortunes, Blount, so we'll get right to work tomorrow. I'll see you here at four sharp.' The Doctor picked up his cigar and started to bring it to his mouth. 'But dear me, Blount, I've been very rude. Here's a cigar for you as well. Let us consecrate our bargain with a fraternal cigar.'

'I'm sorry, Dr. Swarthmore,' Blount said politely, 'but I'm afraid I don't smoke.'

'Don't you? Of course you don't.' The Doctor lit his cigar and took up his book again. 'Till tomorrow, then.'

The Portrait

When Blount returned to the study on the following afternoon, Dr. Swarthmore steered him to one of the two stuffed chairs that flanked the microscopic fireplace, pressed a copy of the pamphlet into his hands and sat down in the other chair.

Blount looked around the room in a wondering sort of way.

'Yes, it's a nice room, Blount,' the Doctor said, 'but nothing marvellous. Anyway, you saw it last night.'

The younger man reddened. 'I'm sorry, Doctor. I was just curious. You see, I didn't remember until after I left. I was looking for your ancestor.'

'My ancestor! What can you mean, Blount?' The Doctor spoke through the smoke of the cigar he was igniting. 'Is there a rumour abroad that my house is haunted?'

'Oh no, Doctor. Nothing like that. I mean the picture of your ancestor that you mentioned in your sermon the other day. You said you had it hanging in your study here.'

'Of course. *That* ancestor.' Dr. Swarthmore was, apparently, highly amused. 'The truth is, Blount, that you've caught me out in a fib. You see, that ancestor of mine grew so ugly that I couldn't endure him any longer. I've banished him to the basement, where no doubt he's frightening the daylights out of the rats. But let us turn to the business at hand. Do you have any questions about the contents of the pamphlet? We'd better make sure you understand your merchandise before we turn you loose with it.'

Blount turned over the pages of the pamphlet. 'There *is* one thing, Doctor,' he said, in an earnest and deferential way. 'I'm puzzled by this stuff about the Nine Witnesses. How come you can't read any of their writing here?'

Dr. Swarthmore snorted and pulled at his cigar.

'That's because there aren't any Nine Witnesses, you

bumpkin – as if you didn't know!'

'There aren't?' Blount's eyes were as big as saucers. 'Then why –'

'Why? Why?' The Doctor mimicked him, letting his own eyes grow wide. 'Because it gives the thing a flavour of authenticity, that's why.' Here he appeared to bring himself up short. When he resumed, his diction was pedantic. 'You know as well as I do, Blount, that people won't buy the thing if they think they're being suckered too casually. But if the fraud's elaborate enough they *will* buy – even if they smell the fraud. Woe betide the man who denigrates the public's intelligence, Blount!' He leaned forward to tap the younger man's knee. 'People resent contempt – easy contempt, anyway. But show folks that you're making an effort and they'll reward you accordingly. Now, people won't be fooled by the Nine Witnesses – not many of them. They're going to say, "Why this is nothing but a cheap trick! That parson ought to be hanged!" And that will generate interest, Blount. These people will talk to their friends – to show how smart they are, you know, to show how they weren't fooled – and the friends will buy the pamphlet, so they can show it off and brag about how they weren't fooled either.'

'That's darned smart, Dr. Swarthmore,' Blount exclaimed. 'And decent too – of course, you want everybody to read it, so they'll be ready when the time comes.' He looked the older man straight in the eye. 'You're a Christian, Dr. Swarthmore!'

There was silence.

'I'll admit, Blount,' Dr. Swarthmore said at last, 'that I was being a little gay with you just now – about those Witnesses, I mean – and no doubt I deserve to be cheeked in return. But there are limits, fellow –' he showed his teeth '– and I will not be mocked by the likes of you.'

Blount ducked his head. 'I don't know what you mean, Dr. Swarthmore,' he mumbled, looking at the floor. 'I only meant that that was a good idea of yours, trying to arrange things so folks will know what's in store. Or at least you'll have given them the opportunity to know. You'll have discharged your duty to them.' He looked up now, poker-faced. 'That's why you wrote it, of course.'

Dr. Swarthmore studied his partner narrowly for a moment, then stood up and began to pace the room. 'I wrote it for the money,' he said in his crisp and resonant voice – which had in it that remote howling or baying quality. 'I've lived a threadbare life, Blount. I've consumed myself on the altar of service.' His cigar had gone out. He crossed to the desk, opened a drawer and took out a box of kitchen matches. 'Now, I know that the pamphlet won't make me rich – even your best efforts can't accomplish that, Blount. But I like to have a little money, a little extra money. Simply so that I can enjoy a good cigar from time to time, Blount. For that reason alone.' He restored the cigar to his mouth, relit it and turned his curiously blank and colourless gaze to the middle distance.

'You made it all up to get money!' Blount exclaimed.

'I didn't say that, did I?' Dr. Swarthmore looked perplexed. 'I said I *wrote* it to get money. That vision of mine was a rare piece of luck. A thing like that doesn't come along every day.' He drew on his cigar with visible relish, then looked shrewdly at Blount.

'What bothers you, Blount, is the fact that the pamphlet isn't entirely preposterous to you. You're tempted to extend it some credence.' He gestured expansively. 'Well, go ahead! Believe just as much of it as you want to.'

'I believe pretty much all of it,' Blount said. 'That's why I'm here.'

Dr. Swarthmore put down his cigar.

'Is that so?' he said. 'No harm in taking your word for it, I suppose.'

They spent that afternoon, and several subsequent afternoons, in planning the refurbishment of the pamphlet. Dr. Swarthmore leaned toward economy; Blount leaned the other way. It was Blount's inclination that prevailed. The new edition, when it appeared, had a binding of gorgeous red cloth, upon which the title (abbreviated to *The VISION of Dr. Swarthmore*) was stamped in yellow letters shaped like tongues of fire. The paper inside was heavy and smooth; it confirmed both the weight and the plausibility of the matter printed upon it. To the portraits of Dr. Swarthmore and the Nine Witnesses were added two photographs with the captions 'Dr. Swarthmore Pointing to the Spot Where the Herald of God Appeared to Him' and 'Dr. G.K. Swarthmore in the Cemetery'. The first picture showed the Doctor as he stood in an ill-defined barrenness with his left arm and index finger extended awkwardly toward a circle drawn in lime on the ground beside him. In the cemetery picture he stood rigidly among the urns and obelisks and was not, at first sight, distinguishable from them.

This lavishness did not come cheap. Blount proved to the Doctor that it was necessary to increase the price of the pamphlet – which was now, properly speaking, a small book – to fifty cents.

It took about three weeks to realize the pamphlet in its new format. On an afternoon toward the end of this period, Blount sat behind the Doctor's desk with a pile of page proofs and a pile of corrected galley proofs in front of him. At intervals his hands went to these piles in order to lift and turn a sheet from each of them. Dr. Swarthmore walked up and down behind the younger man, filling the room with cigar smoke, scrutinizing the back of Blount's neck. Finally the last pair of sheets was turned. Blount's posture became flexible. Colour and animation came stealthily to his face.

'This business at the end, Doctor,' Blount said, turning in his chair. 'About the City of God and that corpse. That's going to confuse people. It's not very cheerful either. Sort of depressing, in fact.'

Dr. Swarthmore stopped pacing. 'Oh? And what do you propose, Blount? You know of course that it costs money to reset type.'

'Well, I do know that, Doctor,' said Blount, 'but all I had in mind was dropping the last paragraph or so, where that corpse comes in. Then we could slap on a new ending, something a little more graceful and encouraging. The saints arrayed in glory, maybe. Well, maybe not,' he added, no doubt in response to the Doctor's sudden showing of his teeth, 'but something instead of that corpse. That's going to be tough to explain to people – and they *will* ask about it. They're going to think that the ending is mighty peculiar, and disappointing too. Sort of flat. All I'm suggesting is that maybe you ought to –' he ventured a wink '– goose it a little.'

Dr. Swarthmore continued to show his teeth.

'That's just an expression, sir,' Blount said quickly. 'Pretty bald – I admit it. It just slipped out. Some of the fellows use it and I guess I just picked it up. I guess I just forgot where I am. I guess –' Blount wound down, looking hangdog.

'I won't "goose it a little," Blount,' Dr. Swarthmore said, his diction vehemently crisp, 'and for a very good reason. I've written it down the way it happened to me. I put down what I saw. Had I seen something else, I'd have put that down instead. But I saw what I saw.'

'Of course you did, Dr. Swarthmore.' The younger man exhibited a propitiatory smile. '*That* goes without saying.'

'Blount, what's this stuff now?' Dr. Swarthmore said, narrowing his gaze. 'Are you trying your confidence tricks on me again? Are you?' He advanced on Blount, his hands clasped behind his back, his head cocked. 'I don't like these transformations, Blount. I don't like it when you assume apple-pie cheeks. They don't become you, fellow. I like it better when your complexion's the colour of a piece of sidewalk. And that smile, Blount. I don't appreciate that smile.' He paced a slow circle around Blount and the desk, then paused to glower down on the youth. Blount reddened, fiddled with his hands.

'I see,' the Doctor murmured. 'Now we have the embarrassed country lout, all knuckles and Adam's apple.' He

73

resumed his pacing. 'Now, how is it that you're such a remarkable pedlar, Blount? I've heard a good deal about you. There's not a farm for thirty miles around that you haven't visited with that cardboard grip of yours. And it's said that every one of those farms has put weight in your pockets. Nowhere have they set the dogs on you, closed the door on your nose, pitched you over the gate. They all buy – you please them all. That's why I've retained your services. But how –' his pacing had become rapid '– how, Blount? How have you contrived to make yourself plausible to every mortal creature in the county? How does it work when some toil-sodden rural lump opens the door and sees you standing there? Is your perception so fine that you know instantly and exactly how you should appear to any and all species of human being? Or do you just sketch yourself in outline and leave it to your client to supply the details out of his store of prejudice and banal expectation? You're less a mirror than a vessel, perhaps, a void to be filled. But who puts the nickel in the slot? Who *at this moment* defines you? Not you, Blount, and surely not I – I am able, I hope, to overlook what I am too plausibly invited to see. So who, then? Whose light is cast through your transparency? Hard questions, hard to get at you, fellow –' Dr. Swarthmore had wandered to the window, and now he stared out at the flat blue sky.

Blount squirmed, making his chair squeak.

'That's just not fair, Dr. Swarthmore,' he said. 'I don't know what on earth you're trying to say about me, but it's just not so, whatever it is. Why, here I am working away like there's no tomorrow, getting things ready so your pamphlet will have a nice big sale and some people at least will know what's in store for them, and all for a pretty miserable twenty-five percent of the net, if you don't mind my saying so, and – well, I don't mean to be disrespectful, Dr. Swarthmore, but I've got feelings just like anybody else and I don't much enjoy being talked about as if I were a fire plug or a fence post or something, at least not when I'm in the room to hear it. In fact, I'm not sure I can go on with this thing unless I get a little more consideration. I really think, Dr. Swarthmore, that you owe me a little more consideration.'

'Consideration.' The Doctor looked away from the window. 'You want more consideration.' He raised his hand. 'But don't tell me. There's no need to tell me. There's only one species of consideration that would suit *you*, I think.'

'I had in mind something on the order of fifty per cent,' Blount said, and he was, once again, as cool as a cucumber. 'You'll remember that those were my original terms.'

The Doctor looked out of the window again.

'The figure's open to negotiation, of course,' Blount went on, 'but I can't go much lower and still feel right about giving my whole effort to the business and not just the half or three-quarters that that paper you made me sign encourages me to bring out, assuming that that paper binds me to anything in particular. Not that I'd wilfully shirk or slacken, you understand. I guess it's the way I'm made: I just can't make an effort that's out of keeping with the consideration I get for making it, somehow. I seem to have an idea – well, more of a feeling, really – that I would be mocking God if I used the talent he gave me without getting a return appropriate to my expenditure, so to speak. Now, it may be that I've taken this idea too much to heart. It may be that I should be a little more free and easy than I am in my commerce with the world. And whether or not I *should* be, I would be, if I could. But the fact is that I can't. I can't do otherwise. I would if I could but I can't. So I hope you won't hold it against me, Dr. Swarthmore, since it's not really up to *me* at all. I'm sure you understand.'

'Oh, I understand, Blount.' The Doctor turned from the window with a face absolutely full of teeth. 'Certainly I do. You're holding me up, you son of a bitch! And it's not going to do you a bit of good, because you've misjudged your man. Which disappoints me in a way: I wonder how well you'll do, Blount, selling my pamphlet outside the narrowest range of Indiana hickdom, if you can't make yourself plausible to the clergy. Or at any rate don't know what it is you should do, what you should make of yourself, to be acceptable to *this* particular servant of God. Not a bad try, really. It might have worked on – I won't say a more credulous man, but a different sort of man. But I expected more discrimination. I decided what I would pay you on the basis of what I thought you were worth. Now I discover that there's less to you than I thought. But a bargain's a bargain. I'll let the twenty-five per cent stand. But try to come in here and hold me up again –' his brows contracted in a ferocious scowl '– and I'll make you wish you had never been born. If you ever were.'

Blount flapped his arms, baffled and fretful beyond endurance, apparently.

'Dr. Swarthmore, I don't know where you've gotten these ideas about me, but you're wrong – you must believe that! Why, I *want* to help you sell your pamphlet – and I'm not too shy to say that you'd be hard put to find anyone who'd do a better job. It isn't the money. Not for its own sake. It's just that I've got to have assurance that I'll be compensated according to my deserts, so to speak, or I just can't do it right. I mean, I can't do it so that pamphlet'll sell well – I mean, really *well*. It's just not in me, don't you see? And if it doesn't sell as well as it possibly could, why, I'll feel terrible, Dr. Swarthmore. I'll think about all those folks not *knowing* and I'll feel just awful. But give me – why, give me even just *forty* percent and it'll be better for everyone – *you'll* see. But if you can't allow me that much, well then I don't know.' Blount shook his head mournfully. 'I'll go on with it, of course – my word is my bond, Dr. Swarthmore – but I don't have much confidence in the result. I just won't have my heart in it, you see. Then there's the printing costs and so forth – it'll be a terrible waste. All of my time and your money for – well, not exactly nothing, but certainly for a good deal less than it could be. Maybe even less than we need to cover your costs – it's hard to say. Anyway, it's up to you, Dr. Swarthmore.'

Making this speech seemed to calm Blount down, for at the end of it he looked as self-possessed as a block of ice. The Doctor stared down malignantly at the younger man, whose prim, narrow figure so coolly occupied his own desk chair, then reached past him to take a cigar out of the drawer. He lit it and puffed hard for a minute, then turned sharply to Blount.

'You're a liar, Blount,' he declared, 'a vile, bloodless, unholy, machine-tooled, kiln-fired liar. But I give you your due. You're no garden-variety hypocrite. You're a new category altogether. There's no substance to you but a kind of embodied greed – no, not even that; greed's the antithesis of substance. Rather you're a vacuum, an insatiability, a species of inverted cornucopia, into which all being and all seeming might flow together and be lost!' The Doctor stared rigidly at Blount, as if ossified from head to foot by the horror of this idea. 'Why, it makes me vertiginous just to look at you. It's as if I were staring into a portal of the abyss. What are you if not – no, wait a minute.' The Doctor scowled. 'What are you?' he said, mocking himself. 'What are you? Why, you're a termite, that's what you are. I could twist you to splinters with my two hands –' the Doctor's hands twitched at his sides '– and accomplish nothing more than the destruction of a misfired extortionist. I have better uses for my energies. Nevertheless, I don't think I can stand having you in this room a minute longer. I just can't stick it. So I'll give you a full third – a third, and not an atom more. And no, I don't expect you to take my word for it. I'll draw up a new contract and have it brought around to you this evening. You're finished with the proofs, aren't you? Then we have no further business today.' He blinked mildly. 'Good afternoon, Blount.'

Blount had already gathered up the proofs. 'Good afternoon, Dr. Swarthmore,' he said, and he left the room.

The Letter

Nearly a week elapsed before Blount returned to Dr. Swarthmore's study. The Doctor, busy at his desk, did not look up when Blount came into the room.

Dr. Swarthmore was finishing a letter to his son, Eliot, a clergyman in Indianapolis:

'Dear Sonny [the Doctor had written],

'Trust all is well with you and your family. Wish I could say the same for myself. That Blount fellow, my partner in the pamphlet venture, has put me into a funk. The other day this reptile shook me down for a larger share of our as yet entirely hypothetical profits, and it was child's play for him too. That's what I resent – the implication in all of our dealings that I'm no match for him. I entered upon this arrangement as a lark: Blount would add my pamphlet to his line, and I would have the fun of watching the neighbourhood try and figure out what to make of it; perhaps I would get a little money – a very little money – out of the venture as well. But Blount has taken hold of the matter in a terrifying way, inflating it into a grand commercial assault on the whole state of Indiana and costing me enormous sums for what he calls his "preparations".

'Why I have let him do this isn't entirely clear to me. Possibly I have the secret hope – so lunatic that I don't dare voice it to myself – that Blount is right, and that my pamphlet will bring us a fortune. Though I despise Blount, he does give me confidence of a kind. Not because of anything he says or does, but simply because he has chosen to involve himself in this project. I've made inquiries and found that everyone here regards him – but does not necessarily admire him – as a perfect miracle of self-control. Doesn't smoke or drink – doesn't keep company – doesn't gossip – doesn't sleep late – doesn't eat snacks – doesn't indulge himself in any way. I reckon that no one as

stingy with his time and energy as Blount is would invest them
in my enterprise – I still call it *mine*, you see – unless he were
pretty sure of a good return. So, amid all of my doubts, I am
encouraged.

'Now, when I say that Blount is stingy, I don't mean that he's
like you. *You* don't compare at all. You're penny-wise, all right,
but pennies is all that *your* wisdom will ever get you. Remember the morning you lost a quarter down a grating? Of course
you do. You spent the rest of the day in grinding your teeth to
powder. To Blount that would be disgusting: an expenditure –
the expenditure of energy implied by the grinding – made without any hope of a return. Blount would cut his loses and forget
that quarter. As a matter of fact, he wouldn't lose it in the first
place. He wouldn't take a coin out of his pocket within fifty
yards of a grating. My point is that if you're determined to
admire money you ought to put yourself to school under
Blount, because Blount has a grip on the profundities of the
subject that you haven't begun to acquire.

'What makes Blount a better man than you is this: *you* operate on one level of paradox; Blount operates on two. Both you
and Blount practise an austerity that would break down and
kill the flintiest anchorite in the desert – no cakes and ale for
you, or for Blount either, and yet it goes without saying that
both you and Blount are innocent of the motives that compel
the ascetic or the saint. To be brief, you two are in it not for the
glory but for the money. Money not spent is money kept; money
kept is a claim on the future. You and Blount share a preference
for the future over the present. It is *there* and not *here*, that you
will blossom like two roses on the same stem.

'So: a selfish selflessness, a self-aggrandizing self-denial;
that is the first level of paradox, and that is where *you* get off.
The second level is a matter of temperature: *you* are cold, but
Blount is coldly hot. He is, like you, prudent, narrow, phleg-
matic, colourless and thin. But he is also, quite unlike you,
reckless and plunging, a brigand or a buccaneer. And yet there

is really no paradox here; rather, a higher consistency inaccessible to crabbed minds. I will explain it to you.

'Blount knows that there is nothing – nothing in the world – that one cannot express in terms of money. All qualities are expressible as quantities, and all quantities are convertible to cash. Blount also knows that he is himself a repository of quantities – he's his own capital. Now, just as your plutocrat keeps some of his millions in current deposits, some in securities and some in bonds and mortgages, so Blount's inherent wealth is distributed variously. He possesses a finite (if indeterminate) number of years, a certain measure of strength and agility, a given allowance of brains. But whereas the plutocrat can sit on his wealth or spend it, as he pleases, Blount knows that *his* resources will be expended whether he wants to expend them or not. His years will evaporate, his physical powers will decline, even his brain will, in the end, eat itself up. There is nothing he can do about it. But he does have this choice: he can dissipate his capital in wasted time, gratuitous activity and idle musing – or he can convert his capital into something that is outside his dwindling self and yet subject to his control. He can become money.

'Compare the audacity of this ambition with your own meagre striving. *Your* imagination ends in a vision of a few handfuls of tarnished coin, rolled in a sock and buried under the hydrangea bush. You will have money; Blount will *be* money. When Blount dreams of a mountain of gold, that gold is himself – and yet the gold is only a figure in his dream, for Blount knows that money has no substance. Money is an abstraction, like the human soul, and therefore imperishable.

'I'm not suggesting that you become like Blount. You couldn't do it. Your sockful of dollars will have to do for *you*. But Blount's elected. He's told me so himself. He has spoken to me, repeatedly, of what he is pleased to call his "talent". What he means is that he's good at making money – he's better than I am or you are at converting his assets into cash. It would be useless to suggest to Blount that the ability to make money is only one talent among many possible talents, and at that a talent inferior to, say, the ability to write a fine poem or to design a splendid building. Blount wouldn't know what you were talking about – but he would smell the heresy in it. To his remorselessly quantifying mind, *all* ability is no more and no less than the ability to make money. A man who sells a picture that he has painted for a thousand dollars is exactly one hundred times more able than the man who sells a painting for ten dollars. So you see, Blount is an absolute barbarian, a very monster of incompleteness. But there's no need to feel sorry for him, for this terrible narrowness and barrenness is the root of his power.

'Blount's election is its own imperative. The rest of us may fritter our substance as we please, but for Blount every expenditure that fails to justify itself with a tangible return is a sin against the Holy Spirit. It so happens that Blount's notion of sin coincides, more or less, with our own. But Blount's reasons for eschewing sin are not our reasons. Blount is no doubt innocent of fornication – but then, there's no money in it. Not here. If it could be demonstrated to his satisfaction that there *is* money in it, enough money to justify the heat and bother that go into the act, then he would fornicate like a dog. For every nickel raked out of the pot is an accession of grace.

'I have put the matter in terms of *sin* and *grace*. Possibly Blount thinks about it in similar terms, if he is so loose with his resources as to think about it at all. He is, after all, a product of rural Indiana, with its vacuous distances and its anesthetized and reflexive Protestantism. But once he leaves this context – and he *will* leave it, and take most of its loose change with him – he may find another terminology within which to frame his faith. *Now* Blount thinks that he worships God. Eventually he may decide that what he worships is – let us say – the law of the conservation of energy.

'Energy, like the Paraclete, or like money, is manifest only in its operations. In itself, it's an abstraction, again like money. As such, it is perdurable, everlasting. And so is money. Thus the total energy in a given context can never grow greater or less in the context as a whole. But it can be lost – indeed, it must be lost – by any coherent *part* of the context, and the rate of loss is a function of the degree to which that part interacts with the other parts. This is why the element in our local context that we call Blount is so careful to minimize its transactions with its surroundings, except when those surroundings may reasonably be expected to yield a pecuniary return. For there is this much mercy in the thing: though a given concentration of energy *must* be dissipated, it is possible to reassemble that energy in a new and more durable concentration. Though a man's capacities are perishable and his flesh is grass, his money will abide forever. Or, if not forever, certainly for as long as the concentration of energy that we call civilization exists to underwrite it. A century from now *you* will be dust, and should anyone have the misfortune to uncover you he will turn away in disgust. But your sockful of dollars will still be of interest to the party, as yet unborn, who digs up your hydrangeas and finds them – and won't you just spin when *that* happens!

'But that's *you*. Blount takes a larger view. Let us say that a man puts his money into a business, which in time becomes a mighty Trust. The founder dies, his heirs perish, his line is extinct – yet the Trust goes on, growing ever vaster and stronger as it gathers to itself the vagrant energies – the vagrant dollars – of the surrounding context. Again and again it sends those dollars out, then draws them to itself again, and with each such casting of the net the dollars grow. Every transaction has its risk – all might be lost – yet only the incessant pursuit of gain can thwart the katabolistic process of loss. And with each successful transaction the risk becomes less; with each transaction there is more that is the Trust and less that is the context that contains the Trust. In the end, ideally, the Trust becomes identical with the context: there is no longer anything that is not the Trust, no inimical outside to its inside, and so the Trust escapes both the peril of decay and the imperative of growth. There is nothing for the Trust to do now except to *be*.

'But of course it is impossible. A single tree cannot crowd out the forest and so itself become the forest, if only because every other tree is asserting its own claim to primacy. And the forest is not the end of it: systems open upon systems; the context is boundless. The thing can't be done. And yet to do it is Blount's sole striving. The means are dynamism and ceaseless change, but the end is perfect repose. He is insatiable so that he might put an end to appetite; but there can be no end to appetite, and so he is insatiable.

'Blount came into the room some time ago, but I have been careful not to let on that I know it. It gives me a mean pleasure to think that I am wasting his time. And in fact I do have one more thing to say.

'I have touched on certain aspects of Blount, but the central problem is this: is Blount aware of Blount? Does Blount know that Blount exists? Or is he merely a sort of blind feeding, like a sea anemone? I would give something to know the answer. Meanwhile, beware: there are many like Blount; there will be more. Don't be one of them.

'But no – I don't have to worry about *that*, do I?

'Ever your loving
Father'

The Poster

When Dr. Swarthmore looked up from his letter, his eyes widened slightly in apparent signification of the fact that he saw Blount and recognized him.

'Why, Blount!' the Doctor exclaimed. 'How long have you been standing there?'

'Six minutes,' Blount said.

'As long as that. I apologize, Blount. Though really it's your own fault. You don't do anything to fill up a room, somehow. But what's that you've got with you?'

Blount, conceding only a brief hinged motion of his forearm, handed over a tight paper cylinder about five feet long. The Doctor held it for a moment, looking perplexed, then anchored the corners of the roll to his desk with his ashtray and a small basket filled with offering envelopes and began to unwind it. A few inches down, in enormous flame-coloured letters on a field of midnight blue, appeared the single word

ARMAGEDDON

followed, several inches later, by

The VISION of Dr. Swarthmore

The Doctor pushed his chair aside with his foot and backed away toward the window, unrolling the scroll as he went:

The SECOND COMING of JESUS CHRIST
The Destruction of the World
The Slaughter of MILLIONS
THE CITY OF GOD

The type devolved into a picture, in four atrocious colours, of Dr. Swarthmore and the Celestial Being. With expressions of imbecile serenity (the Being had been endowed with features and parted hair), they gazed down upon an inextricable confusion of moiling armies and disintegrating cities, while in the midnight sky above them floated the City of God, which looked something like a luminous soap bubble and something like a silver tea service on a tray. At the foot of the poster, in vast black letters, was the date

MARCH 21, 1901

and under it, in crisp, small, businesslike print,

Put your house in order

Dr. Swarthmore let go of the end. The poster rolled up with a snap, jumped right over its anchors, and fell to the floor at Blount's feet. Blount picked it up, brushed it delicately with his fingertips and laid it on the desk again.

'Blount, what is this object?'

Blount looked dumb. 'Why, it's a poster, Dr. Swarthmore.'

'A poster – of course. Now tell me, what do you mean to do with it?'

'I guess I mean to hang it, Doctor.' Then, in a sudden access of enthusiasm: 'Why, we'll put one on every barn in Indiana! You'll see.'

'Well, no, Blount. I think that in fact I will not.' The Doctor sat down, folded his hands on the desk top and looked very serious. 'I'm a clergyman, fellow, not a vaudevillian. There are things that I can't do – even if I were inclined to do them. Every barn in Indiana! What would the milk taste like after that? Now carry this thing out of here. You can borrow the fireplace tongs, if you want to.'

The younger man displayed embarrassment. 'It's too late, Dr. Swarthmore.'

'Too late?'

'Yes sir.' Blount threw his gaze into various corners of the room. 'I sent the boys out yesterday. Thirty fellows from the college, each with a hundred posters and a bucket of paste. They're scattered every which way by now.'

'Well, then.' The Doctor pursed and unpursed his lips a number of times, then leaned forward and partially unrolled the poster again.

'Tell me, Blount,' he said finally, 'what's this thing over here? This thing that looks like a plate of scrambled eggs?'

Blount went around the desk and stood beside the Doctor's chair. 'This here? That's Indianapolis after the angel pours his vial upon the sun. It's in the pamphlet. Don't you remember, Dr. Swarthmore?'

The Doctor showed his teeth. 'No, but I'm sure it's canonical. And this? This stew of confusion over here?'

'I'm not absolutely sure, Doctor, but I think it's the waters engulfing Babylon the Great, or New York, or some such place. Anyway, it's in the pamphlet.'

'I see.' The Doctor rolled the poster up, tapped the end to make a true cylinder of it and turned in his chair to prop the cylinder against the wall. Blount, meanwhile, had returned to his former position in front of the desk. Dr. Swarthmore folded his hands on the desk top again and looked even more serious than he had looked before.

'Blount, it's time you told me exactly what you've done and what you plan to do. You may as well be candid, since I won't bother you overmuch with objections. It's too late for that. Anyway, I'm resigned. But I would like to know what other enormities you have in store, so that I won't go into a funk when you spring them. So tell me, what is your plan? Go ahead, sit down if you want to.'

* * *

Most of Blount's transactions were simple. When it was cold, he sold ice skates and remedies for the grippe. When it was hot, he dealt in hammocks and palm-leaf fans. The goods moved from Blount to the client, the money from the client to Blount – a process as graceful and nearly as effortless as a plant's transactions with the soil and the air.

The effortlessness was predicated, however, on the acknowledgement of a want. A want – Blount hoped that this didn't sound too peculiar – a want was a sort of hollow or vacancy inside the client. A species of hole. At any rate, that was how he put the matter to himself. His talent, the one he had talked about before, was at bottom a knack for knowing a hole when he saw one. As a matter of fact, he could generally see the client's hole, and the size and the shape of it too, even if the client didn't know he had a hole. Most of the time, of course, the client was either aware that he had a hole – aware, that is, of a specific want that required a specific mode of address in the shape of a specific commodity – or close enough to being aware that it took only a trifling exertion of judgement and enterprise on Blount's part to nudge the hole to the surface, so to speak. And once the hole was out where the client couldn't fail to know that he had it, it was no trick at all for Blount to fill the hole in a manner that was entirely to the client's satisfaction. Was he making himself clear?

'Perfectly,' said Dr. Swarthmore.

So, as he said, most of his transactions were simple. Fly-swatters and ice cream machines in the summer, rat poison and felted innersoles in the winter. It was as easy as sleeping. The task of selling Dr. Swarthmore's pamphlet, however, was a horse of a different colour. The want that the pamphlet was so admirably fitted to satisfy was, as yet, a delicate and half-formed thing – a mere tenuous unease, afloat like the primal jellyfish in the deepest currents of the public mind. Deep as it was, though, Blount did not doubt his ability to coax it to the surface in any individual case. The problem was that he could not bring his ability to bear, in his own person, in all of the cases. Nor could he rely on others to multiply his person, as it were. No ordinary salesman could be expected to put his fingers on the individual client's share of an implicit and collective unease and tickle it up, so to speak, into an explicit and personal dread. At any rate, no ordinary salesman could be relied upon to process unease into dread rapidly enough to earn his keep, given that the price of the pamphlet was only fifty cents and only forty-two cents of that was profit.

'I think I catch your drift, Blount,' Dr. Swarthmore said. '*You* alone can sell the pamphlet. Therefore you must be ubiquitous, and the poster is the medium of your ubiquity. A person sees the poster spatchcocked on a barn, and his dread, hitherto potential, becomes actual. He sits at home with his knees knocking until one of your salesmen stops by, sells him a pamphlet and puts him out of his misery. *Some* might call this strategy of yours naive – even childish. But *I* call it elegant.' The Doctor showed his teeth.

Blount didn't show anything. He was, he hoped, neither vain enough nor foolish enough to overvalue his own procedures. He did not expect the poster to resolve the unease. It might, at best, refine the unease and nudge it in the general direction of the pamphlet. It could do no more than that. Fortunately, it was not necessary to that it do more. The unease, Blount was confident, would find its resolution without any prompting from him. After all, he had not started the unease in the first place and it was only reasonable to suppose that whatever it was that *had* started it would continue to operate until it had pushed the unease out into the open, as it were. In the end, he was certain, it would be impossible to say to what extent, if any, the poster and so on had advanced that conclusion.

The Doctor broke in: 'The poster and so on, Blount? Explain "and so on".'

It would be impossible to say to what extent the poster, and one or two other matters he would discuss in a minute, had worked to translate an ignorant unease into a knowing dread. He *would* be a fool, though, if he thought the progress of the unease was amenable, in any fundamental sense, to his or anyone else's control. Anyway, it didn't matter. Who could say whether the rider directed the horse or the horse carried the rider? Provided the horse was headed where you wanted to go, the only thing necessary was to stay on until you got there.

'A subtle exposition, Blount,' the Doctor said. 'Now tell me what it means.'

What Blount meant, of course, was that he would have to follow the subterranean progress of the unease with great care and be ready to act in the moment the unease broke the surface and became manifest as dread. Let the moment pass, and the emergent dread would either dwindle away for lack of nourishment or divide itself futilely among any number of objects, none of which would necessarily be Dr. Swarthmore's pamphlet. It would take judgement to recognize the moment when it arrived, and it was only common sense that it would not arrive everywhere at the same time. Blount had to be ready to unleash the pamphlet instantly anywhere in the state. Then he would ride the dread as it travelled from its point of origin.

Blount had worked all of this out even before he had approached Dr. Swarthmore with his offer to sell the pamphlet. He had seen clearly that in order to accomplish his several purposes he would need salesmen, publicists, drudges, spies – he would need special instruments of every kind, and he would need them in quantity. But that was a detail: the college was at hand.

Dr. Swarthmore started to speak, evidently thought better of it and gestured to Blount to continue.

Blount's first step had been to round up a dozen members of the Young Men's Evangelical Fellowship – youths whose idealism made them willing to work without pay, though in fact Blount had not told them that they were working. He had taken them, by rail, on a lightning tour of the state, establishing them on the most prominent corner in every town they hit. The drill was simple: Blount led his charges in the singing of hymns until a crowd of the curious had gathered; then he turned them loose to evoke the terrors of the last days – in particular, the bitter destiny of those who would find themselves, when the time came, arrayed on God's left hand rather than his right. He put in a fresh man whenever the incumbent exhorter began to miss fire and packed in the whole business before the crowd had time in which to become jaded. Blount himself wound up the proceedings with a harangue of finely shaded portentousness. He reminded his auditors that the ground they stood upon was sand, which God might at any moment sweep from beneath their feet. He spoke of the imminence of great events but did not specify the nature of the events or when precisely to expect them. Then the collegians jumped onto the train and rattled off to the next town.

It would have gratified Dr. Swarthmore, Blount said, to see how quickly the evangelicals got the hang of the business. He had left them, within a week, to continue the tour on their own and returned to the college to drum up recruits of another kind – his sales team. This undertaking had required a subtler judgement than had the selection of mere enthusiasts, not to mention a promise of commissions, and it had taken him the better part of another week to put a satisfactory team together.

'I understand perfectly,' Dr. Swarthmore said. 'The religious motive is within the grasp of any simpleton who chooses to possess it. But salesmanship is intrinsic to the soul of the salesman. It's a species of election. Isn't that right, Blount?'

Blount ignored the bait. For the time being, he said, he was holding the salesmen in reserve. He had spent the past couple of days in raising yet another force of collegians, looking this time for nothing more than stamina and a willingness to work cheap. These people had been armed with rolls of posters and fired off to the remotest corners of the state. If the evangelicals had succeeded in encouraging certain unshaped apprehensions, the posters, it was to be hoped, would screw those apprehensions to a sharper focus.

'It is certainly to be hoped,' Dr. Swarthmore said, 'that these preparations of yours will justify their cost. But tell me, Blount, what do we do now?'

'We wait,' Blount replied, standing up. He left the parsonage and went down to the station. A wad of telegrams was put into his hand as he came in. They were from some of his poster-hangers and various other agents scattered around the state.

PILOT KNOB IN
NOV 15 2:37 PM

NOTHING DOING HERE STOP 16 POSTERS HUNG STOP TO
CORYDON THIS PM STOP TINKER

FT BRANCH IND
NOV 15 3:15 PM

NO USE STOP TO PATOKA STOP EVERS

WAKASURA IND
NOV 15 4:12 PM

LOCALS DISTRACTED BY CATTLE AUCTION STOP REMIT
FARE TO NAPPANEE STOP CHANCE

Blount threw these and a dozen similar messages into the wastebasket and settled down to wait. Later, a frugal supper was brought in to him; later still, a no less meagre breakfast. But still he waited. Telegrams arrived, at the rate of two or three per hour, only to be discarded after a glance.

On the third night, as Blount lay sleepless on a cot behind the operator's wicket, a long message came down the wire:

SACKTAW IND

NOV 17 11:23 PM

THIS IS IT STOP BRING ON THE BOYS AND DONT SPARE THE HORSES STOP METHODIST LOVE FEAST TONIGHT STOP GIRL BY ALL ACCOUNTS SANE THREW FIT IN AISLE STOP CLAIMED JUDGEMENT UPON US THEN SHOUTED SWEET JESUS IN VOICE LIKE STEAM WHISTLE AND FELL OVER SIDEWAYS STOP CONGREGATION BEAT IT OUT DOOR BUT NOT BEFORE TWO OTHER WOMEN NEITHER AS GOODLOOKING AS FIRST ALSO OVERCOME STOP THREE WOMEN CARRIED INTO SALOON ACROSS THE WAY STOP WHOLE TOWN IN THERE NOW STOP FUNK THICK ENOUGH TO SWIM IN STOP TALK OF VISITATION NOISE IN RAFTERS LIKE GREAT BEATING WINGS ETC STOP THREE WOMEN STILL OUT COLD BUT DONT LOOK UNHAPPY ABOUT IT STOP CROWD MORE THAN RIPE FOR PAMPHLET STOP THEYD BUY AN ARK NOW IF YOU HAD ONE STOP SILLSWATER

The Pitch

This was better luck than Blount had any right to expect. He jumped up from his cot, sent a brief message up the line and walked away to the village with long strides. When he returned, an hour later, he had a symmetrical dozen of his most promising salesmen with him. Each salesman carried a brand-new cardboard grip much like the one that Blount kept under the seat of his wagon. A train from Chicago turned up shortly before one and paused, in obedience to Blount's message, while Blount herded the salesmen aboard.

Blount and his retinue had a two-hour ride to Indianapolis, where they would change trains. The salesmen slept. Blount wrote out a sales pitch appropriate to the circumstances in Sacktaw. There were another two hours in the dim echoing vastness of Union Station, which Blount and the salesmen had to themselves. Blount improved the time by lining up the salesmen on a bench and leading them through the pitch, line by line, until they had it by heart. A passing stranger, hearing the chant of the salesmen in the vaulted gloom of the station, might have thought of monks at compline.

BLOUNT: All right. You have your grip in your left hand and one copy of the pamphlet in your right-hand coat pocket. You knock on the door, and when the client opens the door you tip your hat – so – and put the grip down – so. Putting the grip down has two purposes. First, it reassures the client – shows him you're not going to try and barge your way into the house. At the same time, it shows him you're not going to be easy to get off that porch. You've taken your stand and there you stay until you've had your say. And this is how you begin: 'Good morning, sir – or ma'am – not too cold for the time of year, is it?' *You* say it.

93

SALESMEN: 'Good morning, sir – or ma'am – not too cold for the time of year, is it?'

BLOUNT: This isn't just small talk. People hate to be disagreeable, so if you invite them to agree that it's not too cold they'll be in less of a hurry to shut the cold out – and you with it. Let's continue: 'Sorry to bother you like this – you're probably busy as the dickens – but I won't take a minute.'

SALESMEN: 'Sorry to bother you like this – you're probably as busy as the dickens – but I won't take a minute.'

BLOUNT: 'You see, I'm a stranger in this neighbourhood – came in just this morning –'

SALESMEN: 'You see, I'm a stranger in this neighbourhood – came in just this morning –

BLOUNT: 'and since I've come I've been hearing about nothing except that business down at the Methodist church last night.'

SALESMEN: '– and since I've come I've been hearing about nothing except that business down at the Methodist church last night.'

BLOUNT: 'What *was* that all about, anyway?'

SALESMEN: 'What *was* that all about, anyway.'

BLOUNT: Give the client a minute or two to tell you about it, but don't let him go on too long.

TWO OR THREE SALESMEN: 'Give the client a minute or –'

BLOUNT: No.

REMAINING SALESMEN: (Laughter)

BLOUNT: Break in with a quick nod, sort of knowing and grim – like this. You try it.

SALESMEN: (They nod)

BLOUNT: That's the idea. And then, 'Yes, that's just the way I heard it from the other fellow.'

SALESMEN: 'Yes, that's just the way I heard it from the other fellow.'

BLOUNT: 'And, do you know, it's not the first thing of its kind that I've heard about lately.'

SALESMEN: 'And, do you know, it's not the first thing of its kind that I've heard about lately.'

BLOUNT: Pause here and look the client straight in the eye – but only for a moment. Even if he starts to ask you about those other things ignore him and press on: 'But then, it's in keeping with the times, isn't it?'

SALESMEN: 'But then, it's in keeping with the times, isn't it?'

BLOUNT: Here the client might ask you what you mean. Whether he does or not, say this: 'I mean the *end* times, of course, for the signs are multiplying – and I bet you've felt this way yourself – "that the hour of the Lord is at hand."'

SALESMEN: 'I mean the *end* times, of course, for the signs are multiplying – and I bet you've felt this way yourself – that the hour of the Lord is at hand.'

BLOUNT: No, you need the authority of quotation here. Sort of sing-songy: '"The hour of the Lord is at hand."'

SALESMEN: '"The hour of the Lord is at hand."'

BLOUNT: That's better. It's important to get it right, because it's just at this point that we get down to business: 'As a matter of fact, sir/ma'am, maybe you've heard of the extraordinary experience of the Reverend G.K. Swarthmore.'

SALESMEN: 'As a matter of fact, sir/ma'am, maybe you've heard of the extraordinary experience of the Reverend G.K. Swarthmore.'

BLOUNT: 'Dr. Swarthmore, as you probably know, is the rector of North Central Indiana Wesleyan College over in New Parnassus.'

SALESMEN: 'Dr. Swarthmore, as you probably know, is the rector of North Central Indiana Wesleyan College over in New Parnassus.'

BLOUNT: As you're saying this, you slip that copy of the pamphlet out of your right-hand pocket, flip it open with your thumb to the frontispiece portrait of Dr. Swarthmore, hand the pamphlet to the client and immediately clasp your hands behind your back and take a half-step backwards. Like this.

Now you pair off and try it.

SALESMEN: (They rise, pair off and try it.)

BLOUNT: Now the other half.

SALESMEN: (The other half try it.)

BLOUNT: Well, that's all right, I guess. When the time comes, see if you can do it in one continuous smooth motion, like this, and don't be too conspicuous about it. And say, remember where you are when it comes to taking that backward step. You don't want to go pitching down the stairs.

SALESMEN: (They laugh.)

BLOUNT: All right. The important thing now is to just keep talking. (Blount clears his throat.) 'As you see by the title page opposite Dr. Swarthmore's portrait here –'

SALESMEN: 'As you see by the title page opposite Dr. Swarthmore's portrait here –'

BLOUNT: '– the Doctor's experience was of a kind that has been vouchsafed to few men in this or any other age –'

SALESMEN: '– the Doctor's experience was of a kind that has been vouchsafed to few men in this or any other age –'

BLOUNT: '– and yet I have an idea, given what happened here in Sacktaw last night –'

SALESMEN: '– and yet I have an idea, given what happened here in Sacktaw last night –'

BLOUNT: '– that before long many of us will be seeing what Dr. Swarthmore saw.'

SALESMEN: '– that before long many of us will be seeing what Dr. Swarthmore saw.'

BLOUNT: Then you just look hard at the client, poker-faced, for a long second or so. Then you turn slowly, picking up your grip as you turn, and go two or three paces back along the path or two or three steps down the front steps or whatever. Then you stop short, stay that way for just one second and turn slowly to face the client again – looking, if you can manage it, just a trifle menacing or, better, a trifle *uncanny* – with your eyes fixed right on his eyes. And then you say this: 'Oh yes, that will be fifty cents, please.'

SALESMEN: 'Oh yes, that will be fifty cents please.'

BLOUNT: Say it quietly but positively and precisely.

SALESMEN: 'Oh yes, that will be fifty cents please.'

BLOUNT: An audible comma after 'cents'.

SALESMEN: 'Oh yes, that will be fifty cents, please.'

BLOUNT: Just the slightest twist of insinuation, if you see what I mean, on the 'please'.

SALESMEN: 'Oh yes, that will be fifty cents, *please*.'

Blount's party stepped from the train just as the sun was rising. The salesmen's eager breaths fogged the chill November air. Blount left the salesmen in the station, a plank-walled shanty with a dead stove in it, and went out to examine the town. Sacktaw consisted of about two hundred modest clapboard houses and four or five pretentious houses built of brick. Blount sketched a simple map of the place as he went. He paused for a moment in front of the Methodist church; it had a short pyramidal steeple on top and three rows of tombstones to one side. There was nothing about the appearance of the church to suggest that anything remarkable had happened inside it lately. The saloon across the street had its shutters up. As Blount walked back to the station, the houses of the town, hitherto silent, began to give forth the characteristic sounds of morning: the squealing of pumps, the thump of stovewood on the kitchen floor, the voices of parents as they shouted their children out of bed. Thus Sacktaw awoke into the light of a new dispensation.

What Blount did not yet know was that he had journeyed to Sacktaw in vain. For even as he had been mustering his salesmen, a hundred miles away, it had occurred to some relatively level-headed member of the crowd packed into the saloon to use the telephone behind the bar and summon the village's only physician.

The Stomach Pump

Dr. Henry Beecham, a slim young man with a streamlined blond moustache, was new to the town, almost as new to the medical profession. Yet he carried with him, as inevitably as his little bag of instruments, an air of secular confidence so persuasive that a large fraction of the crowd in the saloon gave up its terror as soon as he sauntered through the door. The people nearest the door deferentially retreated a step or two, with the result that when he paused it was to find himself confronted, at a little distance, by a close semicircle of faces whose function seemed to be to illustrate the whole range of possibility between pathological anxiety and hysterical relief.

Dr. Beecham scanned this display with a cool eye and an economical smile. Then he asked to be shown the patient. The crowd shuffled apart, revealing three common bar-room tables. A recumbent female form, with its feet wide apart and pointed toward the doctor, lay on each of them. Dr. Beecham fumbled his smile, recovered it, and approached the centre table – which was occupied, as it happened, by the young woman whose collapse had started the panic in the church. The doctor walked once around the table, looking intently at the motionless figure there and slowly shedding his coat, which he arranged finally over the back of a chair. Meanwhile various members of the crowd told him, in a fragmentary but reasonably adequate way, about the business that had produced the present extraordinary state of affairs. Dr. Beecham; whose eyes were fixed on his patient, took it all in with a noncommittal smile.

Then he made his examination. The crowd watched in respectful silence as he felt the patient's pulse, lifted her eyelids, flexed her limbs, stared down her throat and applied his stethoscope to a decently small aperture he had made in her clothing in the region of the midriff. As he was doing these things, he had the girl's parents brought forward and asked them a few questions. Finally he straightened up and turned to his audience, his smile intact.

His diagnosis, he said, was food poisoning. The agent of the girl's collapse had been neither God nor the devil, but rather the fish-paste sandwich she had eaten for lunch. He would perform the exorcism with the help of a stomach pump. With that, he took the appropriate apparatus out of his bag, uncoiled the long rubber tube that was part of it and began to work the tube through the girl's left nostril. He did it in such a bland and scientific way that many of the onlookers were instantly converted to his view of the matter. But others were not so sure. What about those things she had cried out in the church? Well, the doctor conceded, it was true that food poisoning sometimes disordered the mind as well as the body. It was a simple chemical process, though – nothing transcendental about it. The girl's utterance had assumed a religious shape because she was in a church. Had she been seized by the poison in another context, her outburst might have taken a wholly different form.

Dr. Beecham spoke so confidently that he irritated his listeners. A sarcastic voice came out of the crowd: 'That's all just fine, Doc, but what about Miss Lloyd and Mrs. Struthers here – did they eat some of that fish too?' This sally raised a scattering of laughter, followed by cries of 'Well, what about it, Doc?' and 'Put away that machine, Doc – he's got you.' But the doctor only smiled. He turned his back on the crowd and began to work the handle on his machine. The girl's stomach made a noise like a sink backing up.

'You people have it your way,' the doctor said cheerfully, talking over his shoulder. 'If you want to believe that some supernatural something-or-other has knocked three healthy women unconscious, you go right ahead. I see the appeal in the idea – there's piquancy in it. Nothing as bald and homely as botulism can stand against it on that ground. But you ought to look a little beyond the piquancy. You ought to think about what all of this implies, if you're right and I'm wrong.'

A series of convulsions passed along the girl's body, and presently a bulge appeared in the rubber tube that emerged from her nose. The bulge travelled by fits and starts along the tube until it was pushed by a last propellant belch into the housing of the pump itself. Dr. Beecham unscrewed the cap on the machine, put his fingers in and brought out a pulpy, colourless mass with the consistency of boiled oatmeal. An appalling smell filled the room, and the people nearest the table gulped compulsively.

'I have good news for you,' the doctor said. 'I was right, and you were not.'

A small man near the back murmured, more or less to himself, 'Well, it's fish, all right, but is it *poisoned* fish?' He looked around quickly at his neighbours, blushed and stepped more deeply into the crowd. No one looked at him. Here was the palpable fish. That was good enough for them.

Dr. Beecham let them have a good long look, distributing his smile impartially among the four corners of the room.

'As for the other ladies,' he said at last, 'maybe they're what we practitioners call victims of suggestion. Or they just wanted a share of the attention.' Whereupon the two women gave the game away, one by sitting bolt upright, her face flushed and indignant, the other by opening one gelid eye and nailing the doctor with its malice. The crowd let out a roar of admiration and relief and swarmed around the young physician, who was wiping his hands on a bar towel, to congratulate him and slap him on the back.

When this had gone on for a while someone said, 'Say, Doc, what about the girl here? Shouldn't you take that tube out now?'

'No great hurry,' said Dr. Beecham. 'She's dead. Fish poisoning is a terrible thing.' He shook his head. 'But I've made my point, I think.'

The Editorial

'Well, well,' said Dr. Swarthmore, showing his teeth. 'Confounded by a quack with a stomach pump. How many pamphlets did you sell altogether?'

'Seventeen.'

'And you sold how many yourself?'

'Fifteen.'

'That makes six salesmen per pamphlet, yourself excepted, or a fraction more than eight cents per salesman. The commissions will not be onerous, at any rate. But where are you off to now?'

Blount had risen purposefully from his chair. 'Back to the telegraph office,' he said. 'There's more than one town in Indiana.' And he started for the door, his expression sulky but determined.

'One moment, Blount. I have something here that I want you to see.' The Doctor nodded at a newspaper that lay folded on a corner of the desk. 'It came on the Indianapolis train,' the Doctor continued as Blount unfolded the paper. 'The train that brought you and your myrmidons home, of course. Turn to the editorial page.'

Blount obliged. The title of the lead editorial was 'The Future Comes to Sacktaw.' When the writer had deplored, in a general way, the extent to which superstition and credulity still held sway over the public mind, in spite of a hundred years of progress in science, education and the useful arts, he went on to narrate the events that had drawn Blount to Sacktaw and then, for a novelty, sent him home again with nothing to show for his trouble.

The editorial begged the reader to imagine the interior of the church on that fatal night: the severe furnishings appropriate to a decent Protestant tabernacle, the sober and commonsensical congregation. Suddenly the pleasant murmur of devotion is erased. A girl – a girl admired as much for her modesty as for her beauty – has risen to cry out these terrible words: 'My God, can't you see what's upon us? Don't you feel God's breath on your backs?' Then, with a wordless shout, she stretches her rigid length across the aisle. Silence. A hundred white faces have turned upon the motionless figure of the girl, and the dim vault above these stricken faces is a cavity of unfathomed silence.

And then, inexplicably, this cavity is filled with terrible sound – a groaning and rending that comes from everywhere, and yet has no visible source. Surely this sound is produced by the beams of the vault, contracting upon themselves as they lose the heat of the day; but the hundred white faces turn upward, horror in every line. Two more cries are heard, almost simultaneously, from widely separated pews – two more women are stricken, and the congregation can stand it no longer. With a low, inchoate moan it rises to its feet and flies to the exit, whose narrowness impedes its escape and so inflames its panic. The people at the back of the crush climb over the bodies of those ahead of them. The communion of worshippers now lacks even the brute cohesion of a mob, but finally it gains the street. A few people recover enough courage to dash into the church and out again, as if from a building in flames, with the three unconscious women, whom they carry into the dining room of the hotel across the street. The routed worshippers crowd into the room, to be followed shortly by most of the other townsfolk, who are brought here by curiosity but kept here by fear. The darkness that presses upon the windows has somehow put the place under siege, and each newcomer is quickly made to feel that he has not so much entered the place as escaped into it. As each new arrival adds his mite of fear, the tenuous self-discipline of the crowd deteriorates a little more – a process accelerated by the presence of the three unconscious forms, each as rigid as the tabletop upon which it lies, and retarded only by the knowledge that there is no place else to go. Here and there in the room, women have begun to weep, and the men have lost their power to act –

Suddenly, in the midst of all this ghastliness, a spare, collected figure: Dr. Beecham, representing, with his appliance the stomach pump, courageous skepticism, secular cheer, light in dark corners, science, progress, mastery, the future as an ascending curve. By a single act free of every trace of mystery, he banishes great billowing volumes of mystery; and the night outside the window is, after all, only the night.

'We stand on the threshold of a new century,' the editorial concluded. 'Should we regard this advent with confidence or with foreboding? Because we have young men such as Dr. Beecham to open the way, the answer is self-evident.'

'I suppose it's of no importance,' said Dr. Swarthmore, as Blount folded the newspaper and replaced it on the desk, 'but I wonder how this incident came so quickly to the attention of an Indianapolis paper? This Sacktaw is a skimpy, out-of-the-way kind of place, I understand.'

'Well, actually it's no trick to explain that, Dr. Swarthmore.' Blount's slate-coloured cheek had assumed a slightly warmer tone. 'Now that I think about it, I recall that the fellow in Sacktaw – the one who sent that telegram – is a stringer for one of the wire services, among other things. I thought he might come in handy to us in that capacity, but –'

'But instead he's done our whole project a serious injury. First those dollar-a-dozen salesmen and now this fellow. A choice lot of agents you've recruited, Blount. I suppose we must assume that other papers will pick up the story. Still, I doubt whether many of them will choose to blow the thing up in the way these people have. Or to interpret it in a way so damaging to our interests.'

'Yes, Doctor,' Blount agreed, with a trace of vehemence. 'That editor must be a regular infidel.'

'Infidel! There's a word. Well, Blount, there's no point in

getting exercised about a three-day wonder. By this time next week we'll have completely forgotten Dr. Beecham and his odious machine. But I think it might be in order to start selling the pamphlet without waiting for another Sacktaw. Anyway, there things can cut two ways, as we have seen. But what is this, Blount? You look even more remote and wooden than usual. Something on your mind?'

'Excuse me, Doctor? No, nothing – I was just thinking. And you're right. It's time we got busy. Things are as ripe now as they're ever likely to get. I'll put the boys on it right away.'

'And do your utmost, Blount – you *will*, won't you? I've received a letter from the trustees. They've gotten wind of our enterprise, and there are certain consequences that I may have to face whether the pamphlet succeeds or not. Therefore,' he added sombrely, 'it *must* succeed. I don't relish the shape that matters are likely to take if it fails.'

'Oh, it'll work out fine, Dr. Swarthmore – *you'll* see.'

Blount spoke cheerfully and confidently, but with a certain abstractedness in his eye; it was this detail, presumably, that caused the Doctor to keep his own eye fixed on the door long after the younger man had closed it behind him.

The Contract

Events went swiftly from bad to worse. Every paper in the state carried the story from Sacktaw; all but a few found it worthy of extended editorial comment. Nor did the matter end there. The press made its way to Sacktaw to interview Dr. Beecham and examine his stomach pump – which had been improved, as the young practitioner willingly explained, by certain modifications of his own devising.

Dr. Beecham, alert to the possible rewards of his newly minted fame, signed himself aboard the lyceum circuit. In the month that followed the Sacktaw incident he swept the state, filling high school auditoriums and even church halls with people eager, or at any rate willing, to hear his celebrated lecture: 'The Twentieth Century: The First Century of Man'.

Thus Indiana rode toward the new century on the thrust of a virile secular optimism. The unease that Blount had planned to exploit yielded gratefully to the thrust – in fact, Blount sold three sewing machines and a pump organ on the Saturday after Dr. Beecham passed, like a fructifying wind, through Blount's own territory. It was clear that the exploitable commodity, now, was confidence, and that Dr. Swarthmore's pamphlet was a drug on the market. There was nothing for Blount to do but change sides. He obtained an interview with Dr. Beecham and made certain arrangements. Then he went to see Dr. Swarthmore for the last time.

He found the doctor at his desk, smoking a melancholy cigar. Heaped about him on the desk, the floor and the window sills were thousands and thousands of copies of the pamphlet, so much dross now. The vividness was already lapsing from their red cloth covers. Confounded thus amid the tokens of his failure, which towered over him on every side, Dr. Swarthmore looked diminished, forlorn and old.

'Hello, Doctor,' Blount said, approaching the desk. 'I thought I'd stop by and let you know how the pamphlet is doing.'

The Doctor glanced up listlessly. 'Did you, Blount? That's very courteous of you, I'm sure.'

'I'm afraid the news isn't any too good.' Blount was grave. 'I've had the boys out all week and they've sold only three hundred and eighty-seven copies. That doesn't even cover their expenses – doesn't begin to.'

The Doctor shrugged. 'It's as I expected, Blount. This Dr. Beecham –'

'You're right, Doctor.' Blount seated himself before the desk. 'It's a miserable shame he showed up when he did. We'd be minting money now if he hadn't. But he's more or less turned people's minds in the wrong direction. You could blame it all on that bit of fish that that girl ate, come to think of it.'

'It *was* inconsiderate of her to have eaten that fish,' the Doctor said mildly. 'Still, I don't think this Beecham fellow can last. There's not much substance to his miracle. People will tire of him and his imbecile machine. Perhaps we can still make something of all this.' He looked around, hollow-eyed, at the tottering stacks of pamphlets.

'I agree, Doctor. Beecham can't keep it up – not on his own, anyway. The trouble is that even once he's gone people will go on thinking along the lines he's laid down, at least for a while. And I don't know that we've got enough time to change their minds for them.'

Dr. Swarthmore arrested his wandering gaze and looked hard at his partner. 'Surely something can be done, Blount,' he said crisply. 'Beecham's nonsense can't have reached every corner of the state. There are plenty of people who haven't heard of him or who haven't been convinced by him. We might not make an enormous profit on the pamphlet, but we can make *some* profit.'

'I can't argue with that, Dr. Swarthmore. It would take an

awful lot of hard work, but I've no objection to hard work in a good cause. I'm obliged to wonder, though, whether my share of the return would actually justify all of the work and the trouble that the earning of it would put me to. Of course, it *would* justify the trouble if there were no alternative. But if there *were* an alternative, then I would have to invest my resources – I mean of course my enterprise and energy and so forth – where my judgement suggested they'd reap the larger return. I'd be disloyal to my gifts – which, because they *are* gifts, aren't really mine to use as I might wish – if I didn't –'

'That's enough, Blount,' Dr. Swarthmore said. 'I'd sooner have my throat cut than listen to that stuff again. Anyway, I see your game. You are sidling, crabwise, toward some admission of treachery.'

'Well, you may call it what you like, Dr. Swarthmore.' Blount was tart. 'You'll allow me, I hope, to call it something else. The fact is that I've made another commitment. I've persuaded Dr. Beecham to work up a little book telling about what he did that night with that stomach pump. It'll include the text of the lecture he's been giving and some other stuff about the wonders of modern medicine and all that. Maybe a short autobiography too – *Memoir of a Man of Science* he wants to call it. Just to pad the thing out. The boys will sell it from the platform after his lectures, and they'll also follow up door-to-door in the towns he's already spoken in. I've approached the wholesale newsagents in Indianapolis and all the bigger towns too. So you see, Dr. Swarthmore, the boys and I will be pretty busy for the next little while. I just don't see how we can find time to handle your pamphlet too.'

Dr. Swarthmore showed all of his teeth.

'You mail-order Judas,' he said. 'You night-school snake-in-the-grass.' But his invective had no fire in it. 'Well, you've forgotten one thing. You go right ahead and pimp for Beecham. When you've made your money I'll sue you for breach of contract and shake every last penny out of you.'

'Why, I'm as sorry as can be about all of this, Doctor,' said Blount, 'but you've got to appreciate my point of view. It's simply not possible for me to get a just and proper remuneration from selling your pamphlet. As for the contract, there's one detail. I'm a minor. Did I forget to tell you? Well, there it is. My signature doesn't bind me.'

Dr. Swarthmore was silent for a time. 'I'm disappointed, Blount,' he said finally. 'I thought you had a motive besides your thirty-three percent. I should have known better I suppose, but I thought I could rely on you.'

'Of course I'm sorry it's ended up like this,' Blount said, and butter wouldn't have melted in his mouth, 'but what would my other motive be?'

'Why, my vision, fellow.' The Doctor was even blander than his adversary had been. 'Don't tell me you've forgotten the vision.'

Blount's eyes grew round and innocent. 'Oh, no, Doctor. I wouldn't forget a thing like *that*.'

The Doctor took a long pull on his cigar. Then he laid it in the ashtray and leaned toward Blount, spreading his hands on the desk top.

'All right, Blount. Let me try to understand you. You persuade me to invest the whole of my meagre resources in this miserable venture. Then you abandon me – go over to the enemy, in effect – with the coolness of an Alcibiades. Your every action certifies your absolute cupidity, your inability to rise to any stimulus except the smell of money. Yet now you tell me – you imply, at any rate – that you believe in my pamphlet – you believe what it says. Now, *why* do you tell me this? I see no reason for it. It can't be that you hope thereby to improve my opinion of you. My opinion of you – you surely know this – is fixed for eternity. So what is it, then? I'm curious. If you believe in my vision, then why this treachery? Why have you gone over to Beecham?'

'I don't know that it's fair to put it quite that way, Doctor.'

Blount's tone was judicious. 'I can see why you feel I've done you a bad turn, but I have to take the larger view, so to speak. The plain truth – and I'm very sorry to have to say this – the truth is that people won't buy your pamphlet. But they will buy Dr. Beecham's, and they will listen to what he has to say. Now, what he's telling people in his lectures is more or less the same thing as you're telling them in your pamphlet – I know it doesn't seem that way, if you don't study the matter, but it's true. You're talking about the end of the world, Dr. Beecham is talking about the beginning of the world. It's just a question of attitude. You're both talking about the same thing, really. But Dr. Beecham does it in a way that has a broader appeal at the moment, if you see what I mean. So I feel it's my duty to help him along, to help get the word out.'

Dr. Swarthmore looked disgusted. 'What loathsome sophistry, Blount. Now that it suits you, you decide to interpret my pamphlet as some sort of allegory. As if a wind-up toy like you were capable of interpretation! But just suppose it happens exactly as I say it will, hay? Suppose that every word I've writ-ten is literally true. Why, then your contract with Beecham – if Beecham has been fool enough to let you sign one – is so much scrap, and you and Beecham and your mutual cupidity are motes in the whirlwind. All this running around, Blount – posters, telegrams, rushing about in trains. And now this latest stunt. I wonder why you bother – don't you?'

'I just don't understand you, Dr. Swarthmore,' Blount said, with an air of pique. 'I get the feeling sometimes that you're trying to get me to admit to something or other – I'll be darned if I know what it is. What do I care whether what you say is true and everything will happen in the short run or whether Dr. Beecham's right and it'll happen in the long run? The future will disclose itself in any case, and there's nothing anyone can do about it. But it seems pretty strange, you asking me that. I don't suppose cigars are a commodity that'll be of much use to anybody either, if what you –'

'Reasonable,' Dr. Swarthmore said, raising his hand. 'That's reasonable enough, Blount. I concede the point. But in fact I'm not accusing you of anything. I've made my arrangements. I'm simply curious to know if you've made yours. Our situations aren't the same, fellow. My cigars are an ornament, an embroidery I've made on a future that will occur – whatever its shape – without reference to me. I'm gratuitous, Blount, my cigars are a dim conceit. But you – you're a young man. The future's your medium, or you're its agent. Therefore I'm curious. I wonder what you're doing to get ready. Are you ready for your kingdom, Blount?'

Blount stood up. 'I'm getting ready,' he replied tonelessly. 'I'm doing what I'm doing.'

'Fair enough,' said Dr. Swarthmore, and he carefully extinguished his cigar. 'Now get out of here.'

The Lecture

'My name is Alexander Hamilton Blount. It is my pleasure tonight to introduce to you my friend and associate, Dr. Henry Wexler Beecham.

'A few months ago, Dr. Beecham was an obscure country physician in his first year of independent practice. With energy, skill and devotion, he applied the resources of a modern medical training to the needs of the rural community of Sacktaw, in his native state of Indiana.

'Now, Sacktaw is a sleepy place – an unassuming place. In such a place a medical man might well spend a lifetime in doing good more or less anonymously – famous, indeed, within the little circle of his neighbours, to whom he has brought health and well-being, but unknown to the world at large. A modest destiny but a worthy one – a destiny that Dr. Beecham was perfectly satisfied to fulfil, without seeking a larger sphere.

'But genius will out – genius will seize its opportunity in the midst of cipherdom, and emerge to astonish the world.

'Ladies and gentlemen, I want you to cast your thoughts back to the fall of last year – to a day in November when the organs of the national press swept the linked names of Sacktaw and Beecham to every corner of the United States and beyond to the farthest reaches of the civilized world. It was no trifling news that the papers carried on that day, none of your commonplace assassinations or railroad calamities, but rather an account of events so remarkable, so *outré*, that the exertions of the yellowest journals in the country could scarcely do them justice. I refer, of course, to the circumstances treated in the press under the rubric "the Hoosier horror".

'I do not have time tonight to recapitulate this thrilling episode. Dr. Beecham's pamphlet, *Science versus Superstition, or America at the Crossroads*, will interest those who might wish to peruse a fuller account of the affair than was carried in your local newspaper. This valuable document gives *all* of the facts in the case, including many that for various reasons did not readily lend themselves to disclosure in the public prints; it is in every way a work of extraordinary interest to the serious student of human nature. You will find it offered for sale at the back of the hall immediately following the conclusion of the lecture.

'For our purposes this evening, it is enough to say that on a fateful night last autumn the peaceful village of Sacktaw – a community not unlike your own pleasant town – was plucked of an instant from the threshold of a new century and hurled back into the brute misery and black superstition of a thousand years ago. The Dark Ages had come again, though it was Indiana in the year Nineteen Hundred. Night had fallen in the teeth of an imminent dawn.

'What was the cause? What brought on this fearful night? A small and circumstantial thing, a misunderstanding, an accident. Yet consider the result! Five hundred human souls consumed in a flood of corrosive fear, drowned in the sinister tide of direful rumour and the panic of the herd! Imagine it! In a twinkling, a whole town stripped of all sanity and reason, all of its civilized arts and cunning – five hundred enlightened American minds, products of the most progressive system of public education in the world – five hundred minds left howling in the dark! We learn from this episode just how shallow and paltry a thing our civilization is, how thin the ice upon which we tread – beneath that ice, the dark and coiling waters of savagery and superstition.

'This is the dark lesson of Sacktaw. There is a bright lesson as well. I say that five hundred went down in benightedness and terror; but the five-hundred-and-first did not. Five hundred were lost; but one was not lost, and through his intervention the five hundred were saved. And by "saved" I do not mean merely that they were restored – though restored they were to their wonted decency and level-headedness. But more than that, each of the five hundred went forth armed against any danger of a relapse: never again would they so lose themselves! Thanks to one man – thanks to Dr. Henry Wexler Beecham – five hundred earned their right to participate in the century they were about to inherit. Thanks to Dr. Beecham, they had become fit citizens of the future.

'And who is Dr. Beecham that he was able to accomplish this extraordinary result? On the face of it, there is nothing remarkable about him. He could be the son or the brother of any of you. He is simply one of the thousands of clear-eyed and clear-thinking young men such as are poured forth year by year from the colleges, academies and technical schools of our nation. No, he is not remarkable. He is one of a type. He is typical, let us say, of a remarkable generation – the first generation since the opening of the Christian era to have grown up amid miracles. Of course, I do not mean such miracles as those that illuminated the souls of the first generation in Christ. I speak not of the miracles of Providence, but rather of the prodigies of Man – miracles of reason, science and enlightened enterprise. I speak of such matters as the telephone, the phonograph and the electric light; of automobiles, elevators and skyscrapers. And yet these things are not in themselves so very extraordinary, though they would have astonished the wisest minds of a century ago. What *is* extraordinary is the spirit of which these devices are the fruits – a spirit embodied by such men as Dr. Beecham and characterized by an indomitable confidence in the powers of reason, a cool fearlessness in the face of the unknown and a stubborn unwillingness to be baffled or mystified by any of the myriad phenomena of nature. It was the possession of such a spirit that enabled Dr. Beecham to resist and finally to dispel the panic that had engulfed the good people of Sacktaw. It was this spirit that these same people imbibed from the young physician's steady example, thereby liberating themselves, so to speak, from the dead hand of the past. It is the same spirit that spreads among us day by day, with Dr. Beecham as only one – but far from the least – of its legion of missionaries. It is the spirit that Dr. Beecham has brought with him tonight, and which he will pass on to you. It is the spirit of the future. Ladies and gentlemen, I give you Dr. Henry Wexler Beecham.'

'Ladies and gentlemen, good evening. Many others have stood at this identical podium. They have told you, some of them, of faraway places and ancient times. They have painted in words beautiful pictures of distant and marvellous climes; pictures, too, of the olden days of yore, when chivalrous knights wore the tokens of lovely damsels in the deadly lists; when bold Luther nailed his earth-shaking theses to the cathedral door; when cruel Cortez forced the submission of the mighty empire of Mexico with a handful of desperate adventurers. These worthy lecturers have told you as well of the ·dusty secrets of Pharaoh and his mysterious pyramids and more mysterious sphinx, that famous enigma in the desert sands of distant Egypt. They have told you tales of the Dark Continent, Africa, with her savages and crocodiles. Tales, too, about the fearful land of the Midnight Sun – the Arctic, where the great white bear of the north pursues the hapless Eskimo across everlasting ice.

'But I shall speak of none of these things, for I know nothing about them. I am not learned in those grimy old folios that tell the lore of the antique past. Nor have I travelled to the Equator or the Pole. I have not seen the cathedrals of old Europe or the splintered ruins of the glory that was Greece. Like most of you, I have never passed beyond the borders of our own United States. Yet I am able to tell you of wonders that surpass anything that is to be found in the rubbish heaps of the world's past, or in the jungles and deserts of the great heathen world, now almost wholly disclosed to us by the intrepidity of the explorers and missionaries of the century just completed. I shall speak to you not of the world that is past, but of the world to come; not of the four corners of the earth, but of *this* corner of the earth – I mean this particular place, this town. *Your* town.

'Ladies and gentlemen, I ask you to exert your imaginations. Imagine, if you will, that you are your own posterity. A hundred years have passed. We are gathered in this identical hall – now grown mossy and historical – on the evening of the thirty-first day of December in the year Two Thousand. The year Two Thousand, ladies and gentlemen! It is no mere century that now draws to a close, but a whole millennium – a period of one *thousand* years. Yet in saying this, we are perhaps still short of doing justice to the dignity and portentousness of the moment at hand, for it was held by many of the greatest philosophers of antiquity that history discloses itself in epochs of *two* thousand years – that every second millennium introduces a new dispensation, a new ordering of the world's affairs. We may smile at the quaintness of the notion; indeed, it seems simple-minded to suppose that time should tie itself up into such orderly parcels. And yet, when we cast our minds back over those two thousands of years, and consider where we stand today, it is difficult *not* to conclude that what we await here, as midnight rushes toward us, westward across the sea, is the most significant moment in the history of mankind since the instant of God's incarnation in human flesh.

'We achieve this stupendous conviction because we are able to see, from the eminence upon which we stand, the whole sum and tendency of those twenty expired centuries. We stand, as it were, upon a flight of twenty steps – indeed, we stand now upon the last step but one, and with one foot poised on the landing. The centuries fall away behind us, vertiginous and steep. At the bottom of the flight nothing is distinct – all is murk and swirling vapour, cloud-rack and confusion. It is no use trying to see what lies down there; we soon give up the effort and allow our gaze to withdraw up the flight. Yet our eyes must pass over more than half the steps before there is any thinning of the pall; three-quarters of the steps have slid beneath our gaze before there is any substantial access of light.

But the light, once it is established, comes on rapidly. Each of the topmost two or three steps is bathed in a radiance that would absolutely blind any denizen of the lower steps – but which is nothing remarkable to us, who are accustomed to the brightest light of all.

'We observe by the light of the last few steps that each of them is overwhelmingly higher than any that have come before it. We see, in other words, that each of the last few centuries of our epoch surpasses the whole sum of its predecessors. As the nineteenth step – the nineteenth century – exceeds in progress all previous centuries combined, so our own step – the twentieth – has overwhelmingly transcended the highest achievements of the nineteenth.

'Indeed, how primitive that vaunted century looks to us now. We would not belittle its accomplishments – for after all, the achievements of our own century are founded on them – but with the best will in the world we cannot but condescend to it. It is simply that we stand on such an eminence above it; everything below can scarcely look otherwise than trifling and mean.

'Here, for example, is your proud citizen of the latter end of the nineteenth century, gesturing grandly toward the arrayed wonders of his age – his steam locomotives, his telephones, his electric light, his sewing machines and typewriters. But our distance from him renders his gestures meaningless, if not ridiculous; they signify no more to us than do the squirmings of a bacterium in the field of a microscope. What is a steam locomotive to *us*, who can belt the equator in a day, when we want to? Yes, and never touch the ground while we're at it, for in spite of the nay-sayings and the head-shakings of the professors, who declared that nature wouldn't stand it, we have long since learned to fly. Cunning apparatuses of wire and canvas, powered by an electric engine no bigger than your hat, have made every man an aeronaut. In fact, many of us have come here tonight in contrivances of this kind, flocking in from the suburbs of the town, which has now grown into a great and cleanly city.

'But more of that anon. Meanwhile here's our nineteenth-century gent strutting up and down and waving a little gaudy rag of bunting. What's our microbe on about? Why, he's congratulating himself for the country's recent acquisition of a few millions of unblessed coloured folk in out-of-the-way places like Cuba and the Philippines. Soon now, he boasts, we'll add Mexico and Guatemala to the bag. What the insect doesn't know – can't know – is that before his grandsons are in long pants the whole world will have been united, under the aegis of the Anglo-Saxon race, into a single grand universal republic, and that all of the dusky tribes of the earth will have gone to school under an army of educators and missionaries – an enterprise against which the great eleemosynary adventures of the nineteenth century will show as the timid reconnoitering of a scouting party – a mere probing of the outermost pickets of heathenism and benightedness.

'But darkness did not yield its empire graciously. The wars of the twentieth century reduced all of the wars of all of the other centuries to a damp squib. Our nineteenth-century termite sets himself to strutting again, this time to brag about his torpedo destroyers and battle cruisers, his rapid-fire howitzers and Hotchkiss guns, his cordite and phosphorus shells, siege mortars and hand-grenades. Some pretty nasty goods, it is true, but a Sunday-school's picnic outfit to the arsenals consumed in this, the most ghastly and splendid of centuries. Ghastly beyond compare, as anyone can testify who has seen the operations upon flesh and property of an electromagnetic cannon or a drone aerostat laden with radium bombs; yet splendid too, splendid to a degree that strains all of the riveting of that word, for *our* wars have exhausted the very notion and concept of war. War has used itself up, and may be turned out of the dictionary. The world emerged from war one single commonwealth, Christian in its religion and liberal in its institutions, lastingly and forever at peace. All men, black and white, red and yellow and brown, were now truly brothers, constrained no longer to war against and enslave one another, but free – free at last – to turn their energies to mankind's proper work: the conquest of nature and death.

'Here at last was a worthy warfare for a human race at last grown to manhood. The ancient woes of our species were now attacked with a vigour and a purposefulness unimaginable in those centuries when all but a handful of the world's collective brain was distracted by war or enclouded in ignorance. Problems that had seemed eternal – that men had learned to take for granted as necessary consequences of life, perhaps as the very matter of life – these problems now vanished like graveyard spooks at the first touch of dawn. The Four Horsemen had tracked their muddy hoofprints across every page of history, but here was a new page, fresh and immaculate. War and conquest had received their walking-papers; plague and famine were under notice to follow. The millions of public money formerly lavished upon the machinery of destruction were now devoted to a better end. Laboratories and research facilities sprang up everywhere, and into them marched whole battalions of white-coated young scientists, grimly rolling up their sleeves to do battle with the deadly bacillus. The bacillus, ladies and gentlemen, didn't stand a chance. One wipe of the sponge, and the whole lurid spectrum of disease was wiped clean away. No power of nature could withstand the united will and intellect of the human species.

'And what wonders followed, now that humanity was whole and healthy as well as free and at peace! We have seen, in our lifetimes, the absolute and unconditional defeat of hunger. We have freed ourselves from the vagaries of weather and season: the rain falls when and where we want it to fall, and the sun shines only so much of the time, and no more, as we want it to shine. Tornadoes and hurricanes are extinct, and to find out what a flood is you would have to go to the library. The great rivers of the world have been so set about with dams and levees and breakwaters that the worst of them is no more dangerous to life and property than the fishbowl in your parlour. The blights and diseases of crops and livestock have gone the way of all human sicknesses. Locusts do not exist. The last rat is taxidermy in a museum. Chemistry has applied itself to such effect that it takes no longer to raise a crop of trees than it took to raise a crop of wheat a century ago. As for the wheat, the electric reaping machines have scarcely finished a field before it's time to start over again. Everyone gets his three squares and snacks, and it's not corndodgers and fatback either − no, it's good red meat and apple pie all day long.

'But this cornucopia of eatables is only a part of it. If we eat like kings, it's only proper that we should also be housed and clothed like kings, though in fact our humblest citizen has it smoother than the fanciest king who ever drew breath. Consider the warmth, the comfort, the convenience and the efficiency of any up-to-date house. Versailles is a wigwam to it, and Louis the Fourteenth − the Sun King − a poor shivering savage. Louis had a thousand servants, but there was nothing they could do, short of getting into bed with him, that would keep him half as dry and warm as today's thermo-chemical radiant heating systems. Louis's host of flunkeys and the nineteenth century's Irish slavey have both gone the way of the buffalo. Instead of making slaves of our fellow man, with or without wages, we have made nature our slave − and nature, bound by immutable laws, always gets the job done cleanly, promptly and predictably, without lingering to gossip with the milkman.

'We are touching now on the essence of our century's achievement, the thing done by us that will make the ages stare. I said before that I haven't seen the Great Pyramid of Egypt; nor have I. But I will solve its mystery for you, and do it without a tape measure or a compass either.

'In all of Egypt, there were a million slaves and one *man*. That man was Pharaoh, his pyramid was the token of his manhood and the servitude of those million slaves was the price of it. The labour of the million, the sweat and death of the million, a million shallow graves in the sand – that was the ransom Pharaoh paid in order to redeem his own being. *They* were not in order that *he* might be. And yet it was all for nothing, all a shabby illusion. The mortality of a million could not buy immortality for even one. Pharaoh in his pyramid was no more immortal than a log is immortal.

'And although Pharaoh called himself master, and those others slaves, he was not for all that *free*. Oh, he did what he pleased, lopped the head off anyone who looked at him cross-eyed, slept as late as he liked and all that. But the dependence of the slave on the master is nothing to the dependence of the master on the slave. All of the master's comfort, all of his civility and cultivation, all of the things that sustain him in the illusion that he is free are in fact perfect proofs that he is not; for all of these things he exacts parasitically from the labour of others. Pharaoh was only a kind of gilded tapeworm. His slaves were worms of another kind. A living body lashed face to face with a corpse – that is your master and your slave; but I leave it to you to decide which is which.

'That is the tale of history. We enslaved each other because we could not enslave that which had us enslaved. So long as nature had her way with us, we had no recourse but to have as much of our way as possible with one another. The scientific and technical ingenuity of our species was slow to exert itself; but insofar as the exertion was made, to just that extent did we grope our way toward freedom. Indeed, the progress of the centuries may be measured in terms of the diminishing ratio of slaves to masters: whereas it took a million slaves to make one Pharaoh, by the end of the nineteenth century it required only a few thousand Bohunks to constitute a single Chicago pork baron. This was advancement of a sort, and not to be despised.

'Only in our own time, however, has the ratio collapsed to unity. Whereas formerly a million were enslaved so that one man might think himself free, a thousand made brutes so that one might be a man – or, at least, the simulacrum of a man – we are now all of us free to be men. Really free and really men, our *own* men, giving freely *of* ourselves out of the ever-renewing well of a confident and autonomous selfhood, rather than giving *up* ourselves, grudgingly but irrevocably, out of fear, servility or animal necessity. Our flesh is fed and secure, our beast is nurtured; that much we may take for granted, and turn our energies to ends more worthy of them. We may leave the cultivation of our fields to the machines and devote our time to the cultivation of ourselves – yes, and do it with a cleaner conscience than any dilettante aristocrat or art-gobbling railroad sachem ever could, because we know that we stand upon no man's shoulders, but upon our own two feet.

'This, then, is the great work we have wrought. This is the consummation of the centuries. History has scrolled itself up. We stand at the world's end.'

Dr. Beecham took a drink of water.

'Well, that's just fine, isn't it? But what do we do,*now?* How do we put in the time? Here's your town – your city, I should say. The old town has been levelled to the ground, and in its place stands a brand-new community of purely rational design, self-contained and self-sustaining. Nothing slapdash or jerry-built about *this* town – everything fits, everything works, nothing ever goes wrong. And it takes next to nothing to keep the thing going – a little oil here, a bolt tightened there, a look at the gauges now and then. The whole business doesn't take ten minutes out of anyone's day.

'So what shall we do? I say that we're free to cultivate ourselves, but what does that mean? Are we supposed to sit around and read books all day? That's all very well, but I defy you to find me the man, barring the odd professor or so, who can keep up *that* activity day in and day out. In any case, what is there to read about? History? Who wants to wade in that cesspool any more? History is something we've just finished getting shut of.

Philosophy? A cure for insomnia. Novels? Very nice to read about the lives of make-believe people, but what about our own, real lives? What do we do with *them?* Well, we could all become artists – painters and poets and the like. Every man his own Milton or Michael Angelo! But the plain fact is that most of us aren't cut out for it. Even if we did educate the whole population up into a host of artistic geniuses, where's that host going to find the matter for its art? Art trades in conflict – clean out of stock. Art thrives on passion and morbid emotion – we know better. Art battens on heroics, tragedy, error and uproar – not in style. Art dotes on everything mazy and confused – all gone. Not art, then, but what? Fishing? Star-gazing? Or should we all just settle down and *collect stamps?*

'But this is ridiculous. We're a *doing* people. We didn't get where we are by twiddling our thumbs. Let the dreamers and the layabouts doze over their books and daub their canvases. *Our* hands and brains itch for something to *do.* Nor should we be puzzled to find work for them. All we have to do is adjust our thinking a little.

'You see, we've gotten caught up in the notion – very gratifying in its way – that everything's settled. No wars, no hunger, no disease. People have been wrapped up for so long in the job of putting an end to these matters that they haven't been able to look beyond them. Well, we *have* put an end to them, and the temptation is to let it go at that. But suppose we look at the thing from another angle. We've cleared away all of the rubbish of all of the centuries. For the first time since Adam, we have a chance to take a cold, hard look at the lay of the land. What's the real nature of the landscape that contains us? Where, precisely, do we stand?

'I said before that we're the first of the world's generations with some reason to call itself free. That's true – as far as it goes. But in what does this freedom consist? Well, I've said that too: we're free of one another. No masters, no slaves. A universal democracy. But what's the basis of this democracy? A boundless material prosperity. Whence comes this prosperity? From a rapid progress in science and invention. What are science and invention? They may be defined as the illumination of the laws of nature and the turning of those laws to human ends.

'Now mark what I've said: the turning of those laws to human ends. There's been a lot of loose talk – I've indulged in a little of it myself tonight – a lot of talk about how we've conquered nature – dragged her by the hair through the marketplace, as it were. Well, let me set you straight: we've done nothing of the kind. Nature has set the terms. All we've managed to do, in this golden century of ours, is to make the best possible deal for ourselves under those terms. But the basis of our relations with nature hasn't changed since we came down from the trees. It is now as it has always been: nature dictates, we jump.

'Oh, it's easy to think otherwise. You go for a picnic in the country: trees, flowers, birds, boulders, meandering streams and so forth. You return to the city: glass, asphalt, electric lights, steam radiators, what-have-you. Well, you say, they're like two rival creations – nothing in common. Wrong. There's nothing in the city, nothing in the whole realm of human contrivance, that hasn't been wrought in utter bondage to the adamantine laws of nature – laws that we can learn to play off against one another, but from whose final consequences no magic, craft, science or cunning can save us. We're as foolish as that poor dried rat of a Pharaoh in his pyramid if we think otherwise.

'And what are those final consequences? We shouldn't have to ask. Everything in nature tends toward a single conclusion. All of the laws of nature reduce to a single law. The final law of nature is death.

'Death, my friends. Even as you sit here before me, each of you is rushing headlong toward his grave. Nothing we've done, in this century or any other, can avert that catastrophe for a single one of you. Oh, we've become masters at the art of delay. We know a hundred ways to drag our feet. Famine and war and so forth no longer shorten our lives. It's no longer a matter of remark for a man to live a hundred years. We die all the same. We may be free in any other respect you might care to name, but we are still the branded slaves of death.

'We and all of our works. There is but one thing that is *of* us, one thing that we have, that is exempt from this rule of ruin. That thing is – Thought. Thinkers perish, but a Thought, once given utterance, lingers in the air forever. The whole enmity and malice of nature cannot knock a chip off it. And just as all of nature's laws reduce to the law of death, so we may say that all Thought reduces to a single Idea: the Idea of immortality.

'This is the root of all of our striving. All of our wit and labour go, as they have always gone, toward the substantiation of the insubstantial Idea. And it has all been in vain – absolutely in vain. The pyramids, the cathedrals, the shining cities. As futile as an old maid's cosmetics or Pharaoh's mummy-cloth. It couldn't be otherwise. We are still slaves, absolute chattels, and Pharaoh did not use *his* slaves as cruelly as nature uses us day by day. This is what we know – have always known. The difference is that now we have no choice but to know it. And in the face of such a knowledge we can even grow nostalgic for the old days of turmoil and woe. We would almost have the Four Horsemen back, if we knew their forwarding address.

'But there is no going back, no hiding it. We can no longer plead more pressing business. There is only one business left to us now. We really have no choice.

'We embark now upon the longest and most rigorous of all human enterprises, opening an epoch that will achieve *its* consummation not in two thousand years or twenty thousand, but that will find its end at last. What a light will shine on *that* day, my friends! Our light is anthracite darkness to it.

'Still, we have gained this much: we know now what we must do. Our task is to discover the means to do it. Those means are unimaginable to us now. But a program for seeking them is not. First we must track down and identify every single fact about nature, every wrinkle, every loophole, every dirty trick and confidence-game. Then, when we have brought light to all of nature's dingy corners, and turned all of the skeletons out of all of her closets – then we must put it together and see how it lies. In time, we shall have reduced the whole to utter certitude, and nature's most devious corkscrew turn will be no more to us than a walk around the corner. Then, and only then (and a thousand centuries may have passed), shall we take the final leap. The manner of this leap, as I have said, lies far beyond our present imagining. But make it we shall. And this leap will not merely defy nature and her laws: it will abolish them. We shall make a new universe out of whole cloth. We shall live forever.'

The Votive Cigar

A day or two after his final interview with Blount, Dr. Swarthmore appeared on the doorstep of his only child, the Reverend Eliot Brattle Swarthmore. Eliot was the pastor of a Primitive Methodist congregation in Indianapolis.

'It's me, Sonny,' the Doctor said, as Eliot opened the door. 'Your poor old father. Discharged, disgraced and dispossessed. Amen.'

Eliot was sorry to see him – not, it should be said, because he was scandalized by the old man's foolishness in the matter of the pamphlet, but because he feared that this visit would cost him money.

Eliot had a genius for parsimony. He knew by instinct whether the minutest circumstance would gain or lose money for him. If his wife bought a bar of soap at the grocery, he knew – though he had never studied the matter – that it was not the cheapest bar of its weight to be bought in Indianapolis. This knowledge manifested itself as an ineffable pang, a small, exquisite pain like the lightest nick of a razor. Back to the store his wife would go, to exchange the soap; and only when she returned, with the bargain soap in her string bag and two tears of humiliation squeezed out upon her lower eyelids – only then would Eliot's pain ease away, the cut grow whole again.

But if the extravagance could not be reversed – if the grocer would not take back the soap – then Eliot's suffering would endure forever. Still, soap was a trifle. There were greater extravagances and larger volumes of pain. Eliot's marriage, or rather the cost of setting up a household, had fallen on his limbs like a cleaver. Duty had compelled the expenditure, but it was agony to know that if his wife died the goods bought on her account would fetch only second-hand prices. Day by day, as the value of his chattels declined, the edge of his pain grew more ragged and hurtful. The most melancholy token of decay, Eliot knew, was depreciation. Depreciation was the pecuniary expression of decay.

With the passage of time, the memory of various outrages against his purse acquired the paralysing force of nostalgia. Thus Eliot would be struck motionless in his pulpit, his mouth slack and his throat crammed with undelivered sermon, his mind fetched suddenly back, with a kind of sinking sweetness, upon a bright and imperishable dime – a dime that he had carried in his fist all one day when he was a child, only to open his hand at last and find it gone. Or he recalled the starchy banknotes that he had pinned to his briefs when, as very young man, he had left his father's house and gone to Indianapolis; recalled further how he had awakened the next morning to find himself (with no memory of course of how he had come to be there) in a squalid room that smelled faintly of rosewater, his money and underwear gone.

Eliot's private being had been so severely cropped and pruned and perforated by a thousand such episodes of loss that it was now no bigger than a clam. He moved with the stiff, lugubrious carriage of a veteran of the Indian wars, his flesh full of unretrieved bullets and unexcavated arrowheads. His demeanour was resentful and morose, and it was a blight on his family's happiness when he came into the room.

Now his father had appeared – for a visit, he said. But Eliot, as he looked past Dr. Swarthmore to the street, where a quantity of luggage was being unloaded from a van, was advised by his instincts that he now stood to lose the clearest gain he had made in his life: the gain represented by the twenty years during which his father had supported *him*.

As it happened, Dr. Swarthmore lived in his son's house for thirty years, so Eliot was the loser by a decade. In the course of those years, Eliot's own children grew up and went away, and his wife died. Eliot scarcely noted these departures. A year or two after the last of them, he surrendered his pulpit and devoted himself to the management of his many small investments, no one of which yielded enough income to support a cat. In order to subsist and yet not touch his capital, the now middle-aged Eliot turned to the cultivation of his back yard. Henceforth the Swarthmores, father and son, survived largely on vegetables. Eliot, who had a theory of nutrition, favoured the bulky greens and the crisp, acidic root of the turnip, eaten raw.

On a small rise of ground behind his garden, Eliot assembled some discarded storm windows into a kind of miniature greenhouse or cucumber frame. On any sunny morning, winter or summer, he could be seen to creep through a low opening at one end of this contrivance, wearing only a pair of towels. One towel preserved his modesty. The other was twisted about his head to keep the sun from baking his brains. When he emerged two or three hours later, staggering slightly, with sweat dripping from his moustaches and the lizard-like tan of his stringy torso set off by the two white towels, he looked like a Muslim saint at the end of Ramadan. In fact, he had been engaged in nothing more exalted than a mental inventory of the rags, bottles, cans, newspapers, string, coathangers and burned-out lightbulbs that he had looted from the neighbours' trash and heaped up in various rooms of the house. Nothing that now came into his hand ever left it again.

His father, meanwhile, spent most of his time in looking at the street. When the weather was not too cold, he sat in a chair on the front porch. An ashtray and a box of inferior cigars stood on a little rattan table at his elbow.

With the approach of winter, Dr. Swarthmore reestablished his chair behind the front window in the parlour, at a point just five or six feet to the rear of the space he had occupied on the porch. His attitude in both settings was so immobile that it was hard to believe he had moved at all – maybe the house had crept forward to enclose him. In any case, nothing happened on the street in the course of those thirty years that he had any excuse for missing.

The street was a quiet one. There were no events to speak of, but there were changes. The clothing of the pedestrians changed, automobiles appeared in ever greater numbers and the automobiles too changed from year to year. The Doctor welcomed the changes but did not try to make sense of them. The fact was, he had no curiosity. The particulars of the changes that came to the street did not interest him. What interested him was the circumstance that there was, after all, change. There was change, but he did not change. The street was in time. The Doctor, on his porch, was out of time. That was good enough for him. Sometimes, just to amuse himself, he made an effort to believe that the changes were cumulative; that they implied a tendency and hence an outcome, whatever this outcome might prove to be. As a rule, however, he was content to believe that the changes were arbitrary and that they led nowhere.

On a still and monochromatic afternoon in November, Dr. Swarthmore, now in his ninety-first year, watched the street from his usual place on the porch. The air, though motionless, was chilly, and the Doctor had wrapped himself in his overcoat and spread a blanket over his lap. The lawns, the sidewalks and the street itself were covered with the big, brittle leaves of the oaks that stood in every yard. The leaves were exactly the colour of the wrapper of Dr. Swarthmore's cigar. No one and nothing – neither man, woman, child, dog nor automobile – moved in the street.

Presently the Doctor laid aside his cigar. Its smoke rose from the ashtray on the table in a slender, unvarying column. Beyond the roofs of the houses across the street stood half a dozen analogous columns – the aspiring debris of just so many leaf fires, the smell of which informed every atom of the cold and faintly tarnished air. The smokes ascended to and were lost in a sky whose inner curve did not appear to reach much higher than the tops of the trees.

Dr. Swarthmore cleared his throat. 'Who knoweth the spirit

of man that goeth upward,' he said aloud, 'and the spirit of the beast that goeth downward to the earth?' No one heard him. Eliot was inside the house, deep in a new scheme for saving money. It had occurred to him that in winter the house lost a great deal of heat through its windows. The way to keep the heat, he had decided, was to cover the windows with cardboard, and that was what he was doing. Filial piety obliged him to leave the window in the parlour uncovered, so that when winter came his father could maintain his endless scrutiny of the street. The gesture was superfluous. Darkness fell, and the Doctor did not come in off the porch. Eliot went out to see what was keeping him and discovered that the old man was dead. So he covered the parlour window too.

Acknowledgements

I have reasons connected with this book to be grateful to Peter Bissell, Steven Heighton, John Metcalf, Joseph Morlan, Barry Munger and Kent Nussey. My wife, Gail Scala, knows the extent of my gratitude to her.

I am also grateful to the Ontario Arts Council, which provided me with a Works in Progress Grant for the completion of the book.

JUSTINE SCALA

Alexander Scala was born in New York City and lives in Kingston, Ontario. He wrote numerous essays and articles for the *Kingston Whig-Standard Magazine*, now extinct. His book, *Under the Sun: Essays*, was published by Quarry Press in 1988.